the invisible

Mats Wahl

the invisible

Translated from the Swedish
by Katarina E. Tucker

Farrar, Straus and Giroux
New York

Copyright © 2000 by Mats Wahl

Translation copyright © 2007 by Farrar, Straus and Giroux, LLC

All rights reserved

Originally published in Sweden by Brombergs, under the title *Den Osynlige*, 2000

Distributed in Canada by Douglas & McIntyre Ltd.

Printed in the United States of America

Designed by Jay Colvin

First edition, 2007

10   9   8   7   6   5   4   3   2   1

www.fsgkidsbooks.com

Library of Congress Cataloging-in-Publication Data

Wahl, Mats, date.

    [Osynlige. English.]

    The invisible / Mats Wahl ; translated from the Swedish by Katarina E.
Tucker.— 1st ed.

       p.   cm.

    Summary: A Swedish teenager is assaulted and killed, but returns as a
ghost to find his killer.

    ISBN-13: 978-0-374-33609-7

    ISBN-10: 0-374-33609-1

    [1. Ghosts—Fiction.   2. Murder—Fiction.   3. Criminal investigation—
Fiction.   4. Sweden—Fiction.]   I. Tucker, Katarina Emilie.   II. Title.

PZ7.W12655 In 2007

[E]—dc22

2006037369

The book referred to on page 182 is *Ordinary Men: Reserve Police Battalion 101 and the Final Solution in Poland* by Christopher R. Browning (New York: HarperCollins, 1992).

Contents

monday morning

It was on one of the first days of May that Hilmer Eriksson discovered he had become invisible. Hilmer attended Lugnet School, a small high school that served several villages in this rural area of northern Sweden. He got to school early that day and went up to his classroom, Room 9A. No one was there when he came in. He hung his jacket on the back of his chair, sat down, and opened his school bag.

Hilmer liked to read, and today he was planning to stop by the library to return the books he had borrowed the week before. He took out one of the books (*Huckleberry Finn*), opened it to his favorite chapter (Chapter 7), and started reading. He became so engrossed in the story that he barely noticed when Henrik Malmsten and Lars-Erik Bulterman came into the room.

It was only when he heard Malmsten laugh that he turned around and mumbled a greeting.

But Malmsten and Bulterman didn't seem to notice him. Malmsten sat down in his chair in the corner by the window. Bulterman slid into the seat next to him. Both of the boys stretched out their legs. They wore identical outfits: high black lace-up boots, black pants, black shirts.

Bulterman ran his hand over his buzz-cut hair. He had big ears. He used to have long hair and then his ears didn't stick out.

"Someone should just torch the barracks where all that scum lives," he muttered.

"Yes," Malmsten replied with a smile. "Someone really should torch the parracks!"

Bulterman wrinkled his forehead. "It isn't *parracks*, idiot, it's *barracks*."

Malmsten flushed. "That's what I said."

"It sure sounded like *parracks*," said Bulterman.

"I know what they're called," muttered Malmsten.

4 "Sure you do," said his friend. "Anyway, someone could pour gasoline all over the place."

Malmsten sneered. "Right. Gasoline. Then they would go right up."

"Parracks purn," Bulterman cracked.

Malmsten smacked Bulterman on the arm.

Bulterman laughed. "You have to keep after that migrant scum," he said.

After this, the two of them settled down.

Hilmer guessed they were talking about the housing development up in Sållan, where a hundred or so of the area's "guest workers" from abroad lived. The squat concrete buildings resembled army barracks. He glanced over as Malmsten put the middle finger of his left hand to his mouth and started biting the nail. Malmsten's teeth clicked together when the nail broke.

"Idiot," Bulterman said in a distracted way.

Malmsten kept biting.

"It's important that we tell the same story," Bulterman said after a while.

Malmsten switched fingers and started biting the nail on his pointer finger.

"Do you hear me?" Bulterman asked.

"Of course."

Malmsten switched to his pinkie.

"Cut it out!" Bulterman howled, and kicked Malmsten's shin.

"What'd you kick me for?"

"It's disgusting!"

"You don't have to kick me!"

"I'm gonna kick the crap out of you if you don't stop it!"

"I don't think so," said Malmsten, and began working on his thumbnail.

Bulterman kicked him again, in the same spot as before.

"Goddamnit!"

"I'm gonna teach you a lesson."

And then Bulterman kicked again, but this time Malmsten pulled his leg out of the way.

With glimpses over his shoulder, Hilmer had been watching the two of them. It surprised him that Malmsten hadn't caught him staring and yelled something like "What are you looking at, you freaking idiot?" Now Hilmer turned all the way around in his chair. He wouldn't usually push his luck like this. No one wanted to get caught staring at Bulterman and Malmsten. They didn't care who you were, they'd come after you. A few weeks ago, Ms. Nyman had given them a look and Bulterman had gone crazy.

"What are you staring at?" he'd roared.

"Can you please put away that magazine?" the teacher had answered.

"I can stick it up your ass," Bulterman had replied. His ears had instantly flushed a fiery red.

Ms. Nyman had also flushed, but on her neck. "I see I am going to have to speak with your father," she'd said.

Bulterman had scoffed. Malmsten had shaken his head and slapped his knee.

"You just do that," Bulterman dared.

Ms. Nyman had dared. And two days later someone had spray-painted NYMAN IS A WHORE on the wall next to the school's main entrance.

Malmsten and Bulterman made no secret about who was responsible for the graffiti. They had a big laugh about it for everyone to hear.

Hilmer noticed his classmate Madeleine Strömbom standing in the doorway. She'd halted abruptly on the threshold when she saw Bulterman and Malmsten.

"Are you two the only ones here?" she asked.

"Awww, come sit with us!" Malmsten pleaded.

"Not a chance," answered Madeleine before turning and disappearing down the corridor.

Malmsten pretended to be insulted. "Maddypaddy, don't go!"

Bulterman laughed.

The bell rang, signaling that the teachers would soon be making their first rotation of the day.

"Who do we have?" wondered Bulterman.

"Nyman."

Bulterman groaned as though he'd just taken a punch to the gut. He pounded the desktop with his fists. "I hate this, I hate this, I hate this!"

"Gasoline," said Malmsten. "Someone could pour a little gasoline in here, too."

Bulterman cheered up. "It would take them six months to rebuild this dump."

"At least," muttered Malmsten. "At least six months."

The students drifted in, one after the other. When Madeleine returned, Malmsten yelled, "Maddypaddy! Come and give me a kiss." But Madeleine ignored him.

Then Ms. Liselott Nyman, history teacher for 9A, came in. She was accompanied by a man dressed in gray pants and a yellow suede jacket. The man had a thin mustache, and under his arm he carried a black leather briefcase with a zippered top. His name was Harald Fors.

The class watched Fors with interest.

"We have a visitor," said Ms. Nyman when the class had quieted down. She paused as Hilda Venngarn came through the door.

"Sorry," Hilda whispered, and scurried to her seat.

"As I was saying, we have a visitor," continued Ms. Nyman. "This is Detective Harald Fors. He's an officer from the police department in Aln, and he'd like to talk to you about something important."

Police officers were always interesting, especially one who had journeyed all the way out to their village from Aln, the biggest city in the region. Cops only came out when there was serious trouble. The class was attentive. Fors placed his briefcase on the teacher's desk.

"On Saturday evening, your classmate Hilmer Eriksson disappeared," said Fors. "He left home on his bike around six o'clock to go over to Vallen. He was going to get a towel he'd forgotten in the locker room after soccer practice. He probably never made it there."

Fors paused and looked around the classroom. His gaze roamed over the faces of the curious students.

"If any of you saw Hilmer around that time, I would very much like to speak to you. If any of you know something about Hilmer that you think I need to know, I would definitely like to hear it."

Fors paused again.

Lina Stolk raised her hand. "So he's missing, then?"

"Yes," replied Fors. "His parents started looking for him late Saturday night. On Sunday we began helping. We've searched over a fairly large area at this point."

"But you haven't found him," said Lina.

"No, we haven't found him."

Hilmer had felt uneasy from the moment Detective Fors came into the room. His heart now raced, and his palms were sweating. When Fors announced the disappearance, Hilmer tried to protest.

"I'm right here!" he called out.

But no one seemed to hear him.

Hilmer stood up and threw his library book against the wall. "Can't you see me?" he yelled.

As soon as the book left his hand, it disappeared. It never hit the wall. And it didn't make a sound where it should have fallen—on the floor next to Lina Marksman. The thrown book had proved as soundless and invisible as Hilmer himself.

"I'm here!" cried Hilmer. "I'm right here!"

But no one heard his words. No one noticed his cry. The silent and invisible boy went back to watching and listening.

"Some of you are friends of Hilmer and know him better than others. Obviously."

Detective Fors opened his briefcase and took out a sheet of paper, which he studied before he continued.

"I understand that Daniel Asplund plays on the same soccer team as Hilmer." Fors looked out over the class.

"Daniel isn't here yet," said Ms. Nyman. She looked out over the class just as Fors had. "Has anyone seen Daniel today?"

Several of the students shook their heads. Again Fors checked his paper. "Peter Gelin is also on the soccer team."

"Yes," answered a tall, skinny boy with short blond hair.

Fors nodded in Peter's direction. "Can we talk privately for a minute?"

"Sure."

"That's all for now," Fors said to the class. "If anyone wants to speak with me, I can be reached at this number."

Fors turned around toward the whiteboard, took a marker, and started writing. But the marker was dry.

"I have a new marker here," said Ms. Nyman, producing one out of her bag. With it, Fors wrote a string of digits in thick red strokes. Then he turned toward Peter. "Perhaps we can go and sit somewhere?"

"Sure," Peter said, and got up.

Fors took the briefcase and walked toward the door with Peter following. Just when the door was about to close behind them, Hilmer Eriksson quickly crossed the room and slipped through.

"We can go to the main office," Fors suggested to Peter as Hilmer followed.

Hilmer placed a hand on Peter's shoulder, but the hand disappeared. It seemed as though Peter hadn't felt it either.

They came to the main office. Margit Lundkvist, the school secretary, sat glued to her computer screen as usual. Fors knocked on her open door, and Margit turned around.

"Is there a room we can use?"

Margit glanced at the clock. "You can borrow the principal's office. He's out at a meeting with someone at the real estate office and won't be back for a while."

She got up and guided Fors and Peter to the end of the corridor. "In here," she said, and stepped aside so that the two could get by. Then she closed the door behind them, but not before Hilmer slipped in.

Fors sat in one of the visitor's chairs in front of a desk cluttered with papers and open binders. As Peter sat across from him in the other visitor's chair, Fors opened his briefcase and removed a notebook. From his inside pocket he took a ballpoint pen. With a click, he pushed out the point and in careful handwriting noted the day's date. Then he checked his watch and noted the time.

"How do you spell your last name, Peter?"

"G-E-L-I-N."

Fors wrote it down. "How do you know Hilmer Eriksson?"

"We've been in the same class for nine years."

"Do you ever see each other outside of school?"

"We both play in BK."

"That's the youth soccer league?"

"Yes."

"Are you on the same team?"

"Yes."

"Have you been on the same team a long time?"

"I joined when I was in sixth grade. Hilmer started the same time."

"What position do you play?"

"We switch around, but I like playing forward the best."

"And Hilmer?"

"He likes being goalie, but he's not very good at it. He usually plays defense."

"Why isn't he a good goalie?"

Peter thought for a moment before he answered. "A goalie can't just stand there and wait for the ball to come his way. He has to move with the game. He can even steer the game if he's good. But Hilmer . . ."

"What?"

"Mostly he just stands there and spaces out. At least that's what it looks like."

"So he isn't a good goalie. Is he popular?"

"What do you mean?"

"Do people like him?"

"I guess so."

"If you had to describe him, what would you say?"

Peter remained silent.

"Try," said Fors.

"It's hard."

"Why is it hard?"

Peter hesitated. "He's so normal."

"Is that what characterizes Hilmer? That he's normal?"

"I guess so."

Fors made another note. Then he looked up. "You had practice on Saturday?"

"Yes."

"Did anything in particular happen during practice?"

"We did warm-ups and drills. The usual."

"What's your coach's name?"

"Alf."

"What happened after practice?"

"Nothing special. Showered, got dressed, and biked home. Alf's last name is Nordström. He's the janitor here and at another school down the road."

"And nothing unusual happened in the locker room?"

Peter thought for a while. "No— Wait, yes. Daniel and Hilmer fought over a towel."

"What happened?"

"I think Hilmer had a towel and Daniel forgot his. Daniel took Hilmer's towel and used it and Hilmer tried to get it back. They fought and Hilmer fell. He scraped his knee."

"What kind of fight was it?"

"What do you mean?"

"Were they messing around or serious?"

"It wasn't serious. They're friends."

"So it was an accident that Hilmer fell?"

"Yes."

"Daniel didn't mean to hurt Hilmer?"

"He wouldn't do that. They're friends from chess club, too."

As Fors wrote, Peter shifted in his chair. After a while he said: "There are two weird things about Hilmer. One, he plays chess, and two, he's always really quiet."

"He's quiet?"

"He doesn't say much. Like his mind is some place else."

"Do you have any idea what he thinks about?"

"No."

Fors took more notes. Then he continued. "So there was a fight, a friendly one, in the locker room?"

"Yes."

"Then what happened?"

"I don't know. I got dressed pretty quick and left while Hilmer and Daniel were still messing around."

"So you don't know how it ended?"

"No."

"Who was still there when you left?"

"Almost everyone. I think I was the first one to leave."

Fors put his pen away and zipped the notebook into his briefcase. "Just one last question. Do you have any idea where Hilmer might be?"

"No."

"There isn't a place he sometimes goes, an old hangout or abandoned building?"

"Not that I know of."

Fors got up and gave Peter his card. "Be in touch if you think of anything else I should know about. Don't be afraid to call. Let me be the one to decide if it's important or not."

They shook hands and left the room together, Peter first.

Hilmer stayed behind, seated in a corner chair. It was quiet in the room after Peter and Fors left, except for the sound of a radio from the office next door. Hilmer couldn't remember which room was next to the principal's office.

Memory.

What is wrong with my memory?

He tried to picture what had happened in the locker room on Saturday, but he couldn't. He couldn't even remember what his friend Daniel looked like. Or the towel.

What towel had they fought over?

Then he thought of something else . . . his mother.

What is Mom doing?

Hilmer felt as if he was breaking into a sweat. He tried to picture his mother, but it was difficult. He remembered Dad, but only as a word, not as a person. He tried to picture his father, but he couldn't. He knew that he should know what his mom and dad looked like, but he didn't.

He heard a shout from the playground. Hilmer stood and looked out over the paved school yard from a closed window. He saw two girls walking toward each other, but he didn't recognize them.

This is a dream, Hilmer thought.

Then the door opened, and Principal Sven Humbleberg came

into the room, lugging an overstuffed briefcase. He placed it on one of the chairs in front of the desk and took off his light-colored overcoat. As he was hanging it up, he noticed a red tag from the dry cleaner's stapled to the back of the collar. He tore away the tag, crumpled it up, and was about to throw it in the trash when he noticed Margit standing in the doorway.

"There's a policeman here today," she whispered, as though it was a secret.

Humbleberg furrowed his brow. Distracted now, he put the crumpled-up red tag in his pants pocket. "Really? Is it Nilsson?"

"It's someone from Aln," Margit continued. "He's speaking with students in 9A. He just interviewed a student privately in your office."

"Really, about what?"

Humbleberg opened his gigantic briefcase and took out two binders.

"Hilmer Eriksson has disappeared."

Humbleberg's brow furrowed even more. "Disappeared? Today?"

"On Saturday."

"That doesn't sound good. Is he gone—I mean, completely gone?"

"I'm here!" cried Hilmer. He went up to Humbleberg and slapped him on the shoulder.

But Humbleberg didn't seem to notice anything. He put his hand up to his ear and scratched absentmindedly.

"Yes," said Margit. "It seems like he's disappeared completely." She took a step into the room and whispered: "It could be foul play."

Humbleberg sighed. "It doesn't sound good. Since Saturday . . . Today is Monday."

"Today is Monday." Margit nodded. "I heard about it last night. They were searching over in Vallen. With dogs."

"Terrible," muttered Humbleberg.

"I'm right here!" cried Hilmer. "I'm here, don't you see?" And he went up to the desk, took one of the principal's binders, and threw it at the wall.

He was sure he saw the binder hit the wall, yet it was still lying on the desk from which he had taken it. He grabbed the binder again, and again he threw it. He saw the binder fly through the air and hit the wall.

But the binder he had just thrown remained on the desk.

Nearly choking with frustration, Hilmer threw the binder one more time, with the same result. Humbleberg and Margit didn't notice a thing.

Hilmer let out a desperate sob.

"We have to hope he turns up," said Humbleberg, putting a hand over his mouth to stifle a yawn.

Then Fors returned, followed by a shapely blond student. She wore her long hair loose, and it flowed down her back. She had one earring, a silver hoop in her left ear.

Fors shook hands with Humbleberg as they exchanged greetings.

"I hear that Eriksson is missing," said the principal. "It doesn't sound good."

"No," said Fors. "I just met Ellen here, who has something to tell me. I was wondering if I could use your office again?"

"Certainly," said Humbleberg, and nodded to Ellen. "Go right ahead."

Humbleberg took his bag and left the room. Fors closed the door and sat in the same chair as before. As Ellen took the seat across from him, Fors retrieved his notebook from his briefcase. He opened it to a new page, took out the ballpoint pen, wrote the day's date, and looked at his watch. After recording the time, he observed the girl while flicking his earlobe with the top of his pen.

"Ellen," he said, "what is your last name?"

"Stare."

Fors wrote it down. "You're in Class 9A?"

"I slept late and wasn't there when you told the class about Hilmer."

Fors nodded. "You know Hilmer well?"

"We're together."

"Okay," said Fors. "When did you last see him?"

"On Saturday."

"At what time?"

"Just after six."

"Do you know exactly when it was?"

"He left around six-thirty."

"Where were you?"

"At home."

"Where do you live?"

"Just over in Vreten."

Fors took a map from his briefcase and opened it on the desktop. "Could you show me?"

Ellen got up from the chair and leaned over the map to show Fors her neighborhood. "Here," she said, pointing at the village church in Vreten.

"You live by the church?"

"My mom's the pastor."

"I understand," said Fors, wondering what it was exactly that he understood.

He studied the map. "Vallen is located here," he said. "Hilmer lives here. Your village is in the opposite direction."

"Yes," said Ellen. "Hilmer needed to go to Vallen to get something. He came by my place on the way."

"That was out of his way."

"It only takes ten minutes to bike from Hilmer's to Vreten."

"And about twenty minutes from Vreten to Vallen," said Fors.

"Yes," said Ellen.

"Why did he go to your house when he was on his way to Vallen?"

Ellen hesitated before she answered. "I talked to him on the phone just before five. I asked him to come over."

"Was there something in particular you wanted?"

"No."

Fors looked frankly at the girl in the black skirt and green shirt. "Positive?"

Then Ellen started crying. Her nose reddened, and her eyes brimmed with tears.

"What is it?" Fors asked.

"Nothing," Ellen replied. "I'm just afraid something happened to him."

Fors tilted his head to one side and stared at her. He thought of his own daughter, who lived with his ex-wife and son four hundred miles south, in Stockholm. "It's pretty common for people to disappear once in a while. Most of them come back. People started searching for Hilmer after his mother said that he'd missed his favorite program on TV."

"The soccer match," Ellen said.

"Exactly," said Fors.

"He loves to watch soccer," said Ellen.

"Does he love you?" asked Fors.

Ellen nodded.

"How long have you been together?"

"Since February break."

"But you've been in the same class for nine years?"

"Yes."

Fors set aside the notebook and the pen. Ellen's eyes started to tear up again. Her nose was still red.

"Is there something in particular that makes you sad, Ellen?"

The girl shook her head. "I'm just worried that something has happened to him."

"What could happen to him?"

"I don't know."

"Does he have any enemies?"

"Not that I know of."

Both were silent.

"I think that will do for now," said Fors. "What's your telephone number?"

As Ellen gave the number to Fors, Hilmer recited the digits along with her. Then he went up to Ellen, and from behind he tried to gather her hair in his hand, but she didn't notice.

"Ellen. Ellen, it's me."

She doesn't notice.

He understood things now, with a rising sense of panic.

She did not notice him.

She did not feel him.

Ellen!

He sensed his memory failing. Where Ellen should have been, there was only pain. His head ached, his face and his mouth ached, and neither Fors nor Ellen heard him. Hilmer understood that something else had happened, apart from him becoming invisible. Something terrible. He called out for his mother . . .

Mom!

As Ellen and Fors left the room, Hilmer sank to the floor and screamed; he screamed until he didn't have the strength to scream anymore.

When he got to his feet, Principal Humbleberg was bustling back into the office. The administrator closed the door and took his seat behind the desk. Then he lifted the phone receiver and dialed. After a while the call went through, and Humbleberg spoke into the receiver with a strikingly tense voice.

"Did I wake you?"

And: "I know what time it is."

And: "May I ask you something?"

And: "Did you know that Hilmer Eriksson has disappeared?"

At this point whoever he was speaking with must have hung up, because Humbleberg remained sitting with the receiver away from his ear. He looked at it for a moment and carefully put it down in the cradle again. Then he took up one of his binders, opened it, and made another call.

"I need to speak with Mr. Mattson. No, at the real estate office . . ."

Hilmer got up and walked toward the door. And it was only now that he realized he did not have to open the door. When he thought about being on the other side of the door, he found he had already passed through it.

He was out in the corridor. He walked past the secretary's office and went toward the classrooms. He tried to remember which direction he should go but couldn't. Then he thought about the whiteboard in Room 9A and he was there.

All his classmates, except for Daniel, were sitting in their places. Ms. Nyman was talking about something that had happened during another century. She spoke of how one could know about the past, even though those who had lived through it had been gone for a long time. Bulterman was reading a comic book. Malmsten was half-asleep at his desk with his head resting on his arms. Ellen sat facing Ms. Nyman and the board, where the teacher was scribbling a date. Hilmer looked into Ellen's face and tried to catch her eye.

"Ellen, it's me."

But she didn't hear.

She raised her hand and spoke quietly when she had the teacher's attention. "I have to go. I need to see the nurse."

Ms. Nyman nodded, and Ellen gathered up her things and left the room. Hilmer followed close behind.

They passed the doors to the main office and the staff lounge and turned the corner to the locker hallway. On both sides of the corridor, lockers were set up in short rows perpendicular to the wall. There they saw Alf Nordström heading in their direction. He was dressed in blue pants and a blue work jacket. Around his waist he wore a tool belt.

Detective Fors was standing by one set of lockers at the other end of the hallway. Hilmer watched as Ellen brushed past the policeman with her head down.

The detective let the girl pass, then called out to the janitor.

Nordström stopped abruptly and turned around. Fors walked toward him.

"My name is Harald Fors, and I'm investigating the disappearance of Hilmer Eriksson. Are you Alf Nordström?"

"Yes."

"The coach for BK and janitor here at the school?"

"That's right. Are you a cop?"

Fors nodded. "You know Hilmer?"

"He plays on the team. I see him every day in school. What's this about?"

"He's disappeared. Can you show me his locker?"

"Sure."

Nordström led the way down the long hall of lockers. He stopped at the last locker before a large window that faced the school yard. There was a padlock on the door, and with a heavy black marker someone had scrawled TRAITOR on the front.

"Can you open it?"

"The boy's really gone?"

"Since Saturday. Can you please open the locker?"

"I'll have to get the bolt cutters."

Nordström disappeared down the hall, and Fors stood in front of the window, looking toward the edge of the nearby woods. The sky over the spruce forest was a clear blue. The birch trees were swaying.

Fors caught the sharp scent of disinfectant and flashed back to his own school years. He had played chess, like Hilmer, but he had never been very good at it. His father, a highway inspector, had been an excellent player. He would travel from their small town to Stockholm every year and participate in a chess tournament at City Hall. Once, Harald had gone along—not to play, just to watch. They had rented a room on Agne Street. Harald had been fifteen years old at the time. His father had pointed out the police department headquarters as they drove through the capital. That day, for no particular reason, Harald had decided he wanted to be a police officer. Now he mulled over his career choice. He watched the swaying birches at the edge of the wood and then looked back at Hilmer's locker.

TRAITOR.

Nordström returned with the bolt cutters in hand. He gripped the shackle with the tool and squeezed. The metal broke, and the janitor twisted off the lock.

Hilmer stood behind Nordström and the policeman. *Stay with Fors,* he told himself . . . *Stay with Fors and maybe you'll find out why you've become invisible.*

Hilmer watched Fors reach into the locker and search through books and papers. There were some old tests, a pair of shorts, a gym sock, and the biology book he had borrowed from Daniel, as well as a ballpoint pen, a deck of cards, and a library book about chess.

"Do you have a bag?" asked Fors.

Nordström disappeared again and came back with a plastic shopping bag in hand. Fors filled the bag with the old tests, books, the sock and the shorts, the deck of cards, and the pen. When the locker was empty, Fors studied it for a moment, running his finger along the edge of the shelf before he closed the door.

"Can you put a new lock on it?"

Nordström sighed. "Will there be anything else with the locker?"

"No, but after you've put the new lock on, I'd like to speak with you."

"I need to be at the school over in Hallby in an hour," said Nordström, and looked at his watch. Fors had given his thirteen-year-old son the same kind of watch for his birthday the month before. It had a stopwatch function.

"Of course," said the detective. "It won't take long."

Nordström disappeared again and returned with a new padlock. He secured the locker and gave the two keys to Fors.

"Good," said Fors, pocketing the keys. "Can we go and sit somewhere?"

"We can go to my office," Nordström suggested.

He led Fors toward a glassed-in room at the end of the hall. The shopping bag thumped against Fors's leg as they walked.

"Are there many students here?"

"Four classes per grade."

Fors thought about his own high school, which also had four tracks per grade. He had been in the last track, the class for students who were strong in science and engineering.

"D-track," Highway Inspector Fors had said when Harald came home and told his parents which class he'd been assigned. "That's a good class, an important class. Those who can handle the D-track have a lot of different capabilities." Highway Inspector Fors had liked talking about life as if it were a chess match.

Nordström stopped in front of a slender boy who sat on a radiator next to the last row of lockers, beside the office door. The boy raised his right hand and greeted them silently.

"Taking a break from class, Mahmud?" asked Nordström. Mahmud cast his eyes down at the floor. Nordström turned toward Fors. "This kid is always hiding out around here."

The janitor shook his head, took out a bunch of keys, and opened the door to the his office.

"Step inside," Nordström said. Fors entered, and Nordström closed the door behind him.

A radio stood on a workbench in the corner, playing country-western music.

"Dolly Parton," said Nordström as he turned the volume up a bit.

He took a steel thermos from the table and held it up. "Coffee? There's a clean cup on the shelf next to you. I also have warm milk." Nordström motioned to an identical steel thermos on the table.

"How do you know which one the milk is in?" asked Fors, sitting down in an armchair with a worn cloth seat. Nordström pointed to a thin piece of blue duct tape on the lid of one of the thermoses. Then he took out a cup for himself, screwed off the thermos lids, and served.

"Would you like milk?"

"Thanks."

Nordström settled into an old office chair with an adjustable backrest and wheels on the legs. He leaned back, looking through the glass and raising his cup to a woman with coal black hair who walked past dragging a trash bag.

"So, Eriksson is missing?"

"Since Saturday."

"Nice kid."

"I understand that he likes to be the goalie."

Nordström laughed. "He's no player, that's for sure, but he means well. It's easier to keep him in goal than have him messing around on the field. Some people you just can't figure out. They should do something other than soccer."

"What do you think Hilmer should be doing?"

Nordström offered a dejected sigh. "No idea. He probably doesn't know either. Who knows that at his age? I didn't, at any rate."

"But he's on the team?"

"Never misses practice. Dependable kid. He's even been a Boy Scout."

Nordström leaned forward. "You know why it's a good thing there are so many queers? Because where else would we get all the scout leaders from?" He laughed and slapped his thigh with the palm of his hand.

Fors didn't crack a smile.

"Child molesters," he said. "You know why it's a good thing there are so many? Because where else would we get all the janitors from?"

Nordström dropped the comedy act. "Are you going to find him?"

"Yes," said Fors, sipping his coffee. "Could you tell me about practice the day before yesterday?"

Nordström leaned back in his chair again, so far that it looked as if he was about to tip over. Then he straightened up and slurped some coffee.

"We have endurance training on Saturdays. We run on the cross-country trail. There's a steep hill in the middle of it. We do wind sprints there, five of them. It usually knocks the hell out of them. On the way home, they always want to drag their feet. I get after them. After that we do drills on the gravel field. Most of the kids are out of shape. Some of them even smoke. There should be more rules. Boys who smoke shouldn't be allowed on the team. That's what I think, at any rate, but it doesn't work that way. It's a community sports field, public funds, everyone is allowed to participate. You know how it is. Look at that kid out there."

And Nordström pointed his finger in the direction of the kid he'd called Mahmud. "He cuts half of his classes. Speaks horrible Swedish, even though he's lived in this country for an eternity. In a few years he'll be unemployed. Then the rest of us will have to support him. He'll start a family as well. We'll have to support them, too. There's too much laziness everywhere. That's what I think anyway."

"What did you do after drills?" asked Fors.

"They did some stretching. Then they showered, changed, and left."

"And you?"

"I stayed at the office."

"You didn't shower?"

"No, I changed my shirt. I shower at home."

"Why?"

Nordström looked as though he didn't understand the question. "What do you mean?"

"You'd probably been running, you were probably sweaty, why didn't you shower?"

"I didn't say that I didn't shower. I said that I showered at home."

Fors took his notebook from his briefcase and marked the date and time. "Good coffee," he said.

Nordström gave a sour little smile.

"Did you see when the boys left?" asked Fors.

"I saw a few of them."

"Which ones?"

"Peter Gelin. He was first. Then a whole bunch. I think Hilmer was among them. He has a new bike. I saw him over by the gate. He rode past the others."

"Are you sure?"

Nordström nodded. "He left just after Peter, in a group of seven or eight boys. I didn't see the others."

"How many were at practice?"

"Everyone was there. Twenty-three kids."

Fors pointed through the glass at Mahmud. "Does he play soccer?"

"Not in BK."

"Are there any immigrant kids in BK?"

"No."

"Why not?"

"They have their own team."

"Their own team?"

"Yes. They live up in Sållan, the whole bunch of them. As far as I'm concerned, they can stay in their own neighborhoods, it doesn't bother me."

"Do you usually play against them?"

"Of course."

"Who wins?"

"It varies."

Fors made some notes, and Hilmer, who had been standing in the corner, held his head in his hands and tried to remember his new bike. Did he really have a new bike? He tried to picture it, but his memory didn't work. The pain was overwhelming—in his head, all over his face. He wanted to scream.

Nordström glanced at his wristwatch. "I should probably head over to Hallby now. I'm going to pick up some tools on the way. If there's anything else you want to ask me about, you know where to find me. I'm here at Lugnet School for the most part, but today I'll be at Hallby until four."

Fors stood up. "Thanks for the coffee." He set down his mug. It was a white ceramic mug with a picture of Donald Duck. "Is there a lot of graffiti at this school?"

"No more than anywhere else."

"Do you know who does it?"

"You never find out about that sort of thing. But you always have a good idea who it is."

Fors nodded, opened the door, and, with the shopping bag in hand, went out into the hall, where Mahmud was still sitting.

Hilmer followed—his head in his hands.

His teeth!

His lips!

"How's it going?" said Fors.

Mahmud looked at the detective, wariness in his eyes.

"Aren't you supposed to be in class?"

The boy snorted.

"My name is Harald Fors. I'm a police officer."

"Uh-huh."

"Why aren't you in class?"

"Why should you care?"

Fors looked at the boy.

"What are you staring at?"

"You."

"Go ahead and stare if you want," the boy said.

"Do you know who's responsible for the graffiti at this school?"

"Everyone."

"Everyone?"

"Yes."

"You, too?"

"Yes."

"Do you know who wrote TRAITOR on Hilmer Eriksson's locker?"

Mahmud got up. "It wasn't me, I know that."

With that, he turned and walked off.

"Do you know Hilmer?" Fors called after him.

But Mahmud didn't answer.

Fors went back to Hilmer's locker. He stood there for a while and stared at what had been scrawled on it. The locker doors were all painted in various bright colors. Most of them looked worn and scratched, but Hilmer's door appeared to have been repainted recently.

Then Fors continued along the hallway, shopping bag in hand, and made his way out through the main entrance. He paused again, noting that someone had spray-painted NYMAN IS A WHORE in big letters next to the front door. The slur was painted over in a sloppy fashion, but you could still read it.

Fors stood in front of the wall for a while, pondering the words. Gusty spring winds were tearing at the tops of the spruce trees and bending the birches behind him. A cloud of dust whipped up from the asphalt surface in front of the school, and Fors squinted in order to avoid getting grit in his eyes.

Then he went to the parking lot, got in his Volkswagen, and left the school.

Hilmer Eriksson sat next to him . . . He hadn't slipped in through any of the car doors but had simply entered with Fors, whose thoughts were on him. Hilmer didn't understand it. It was inconceivable. But now he was so much in Fors's thoughts that he was next to Fors, was with Fors, following him and walking along beside him.

Yet he was invisible.

Except to you.

You can see him.

His ruined face.

What have they done to his face?

Fors listened to the local radio station on his way through the district. Two convicts from the county prison had escaped. They'd threatened an ornithologist at a lakeside park with a knife and tried to get his car keys. The ornithologist had gotten away from them. Now the police were searching for the escapees.

Fors changed the channel.

"You ain't nothing but a hound dog," sang Elvis.

Officer Johan Nilsson was standing in his shirtsleeves, scrubbing a pan at the sink in the staff lounge, when Fors arrived at the local police station. The small station was adjacent to the municipal building, and both offices shared a parking lot. Nilsson was just months from retirement. He had been on the force his entire working life. He'd earned a head of gray hair and the kind of nose that betrays a possible fondness for the bottle.

"Coffee?" Nilsson asked.

"Thanks, but I've just had some."

Fors sat at the large table and unfolded his map of the area.

"Eriksson biked from his home here in Lugnet over to Vreten," he said.

Nilsson put the pan down on the dish rack. "That's not what the parents said. They said he was headed to Vallen."

"He was going to Vallen, but he went to Vreten first and visited his girlfriend."

"The parents didn't know," Nilsson guessed.

"How would he bike from Vreten to Vallen if he was in a hurry?"

"The river trail, alongside Grayling River."

"Where is that?"

Nilsson hung the dish towel on the radiator to dry and came over to the table. He pointed with a big, stubby index finger.

"Here somewhere. I'm going to get my glasses."

He returned from the reception area with his reading glasses. They were the cheap, frameless kind sold at pharmacies. He leaned over the map.

"The river runs here. Six years ago they widened the path next to it, built bridges in two places, put in benches, and laid out gravel. The people in charge said that it would become a popular place to go for walks. I don't know if anyone walks there, but it's a shortcut if you're going to bike between these two villages."

"Are there buildings there?" Fors asked, studying the map. "This looks like a house."

"There are a couple summer homes. The chairman of the municipal council, Olle Berg, has a house at the point where Flax Creek runs into the Grayling. There's a cottage nearby."

Fors got up and went out into the reception area. Using the station phone, he called his commander in Aln.

"Hello. It's Fors. I need some men and dogs."

"We have people and dogs around the lake," his boss, Chief Hammarlund, responded. "There are two—"

"I heard. When can I get someone with a dog out here?"

"Tonight maybe. How is it going?"

"The kid disappeared while he was out biking. He was supposed to come home to watch a soccer game. The worst case scenario looks possible."

"You can call Söderström. Tell him that he can drive up to you when he's done by the lake. You can't get anyone else. At least not today."

"I'll call Söderström."

"Do that."

Fors took an address book from the inner pocket of his jacket, found a number, and dialed. He got an answering machine.

Fors left his message, hung up the phone, and went back to Nilsson, who had poured a cup of coffee for himself and was sitting down to snack on a pastry.

"You can have half," Nilsson offered.

"No thanks, I'm on a diet."

"A diet." Nilsson snorted. "You don't need to diet, do you? Look at this." He grabbed his gut right above the waistline. "I'm the one who needs a diet. But that's not going to happen any time soon."

Fors sat across from Nilsson. "How did it go again? When did the parents call?"

"Saturday evening. I was off duty, so they called me at home."

"No one was on duty?"

"These days we're closed on Saturdays, as long as there isn't any big event planned. If there's an emergency, they come from the city."

"So you were off duty?"

"Of course. Watched the soccer game. Went out with my dog, Nicko, came home and saw a film on Channel Four. Then she called."

"Mrs. Eriksson?"

"Yes."

Nilsson took a huge bite, and with his mouth stuffed with pastry, he continued. "You've already heard this. She was worried. The boy hadn't come home. I promised to help her if he wasn't back by Sunday morning. She called at breakfast, seven-thirty, was upset, had been in contact with the station in the city as well, had even spoken with Hammarlund and made a big fuss. I drove out to her place. Hammarlund sent Söderström and two patrolwomen, so there were the four of us and a dog. We searched around Vallen, went into the changing room at the soccer field, and spoke with one of the boys. His name is Ols. I know him from National Guard duty. He's a good kid. He'd seen Hilmer bike from Vallen. It seems as though he biked straight home. Hilmer had forgotten his towel, and his mom asked about it. He told her he'd get it on Monday. But the towel was new and the mom didn't want to lose it, so she made him go back for it. He has a new mountain bike, and the father saw him leave through the gate. No one has seen him since."

"Except Ellen Stare."

"The pastor's daughter?"

"He biked to her place."

"Hilmer's mother didn't mention that. She thought that Hilmer had left for Vallen."

"Can we go take a look at the river path?"

"Of course."

Nilsson stuffed the rest of the pastry in his mouth, took a gulp of coffee, got up, and went to the sink to wash the grease from his fingers. He rolled down the sleeves of his shirt, donned his jacket, and hitched on the equipment belt with his sidearm, flashlight, and clasp knife in its leather sheath. After he put his cell phone in the inside pocket of his coat, they went out. Nilsson paused on the top step under the station sign to lock the door, then made his way to the cruiser, a Volvo with blue flashers on the roof and the word POLICE emblazoned on the sides. Fors got in next to him.

And along with them, without their noticing, he was there, the invisible one, whose name was Hilmer Eriksson. He was in the car as

Nilsson pulled onto the street; he was with them as they drove in silence along the main street toward the river and the trail.

The boy who is gone is still present. No one is closer to us than the one who has disappeared.

We can hide things away. But we can't forget.

Nilsson parked in a lot that was obviously bigger than it needed to be. Nearby were four tables with stationary benches, a garbage can, a Dumpster, two toilets, and a signpost with an arrow pointing into the woods. GRAYLING RIVER: 2 KILOMETERS.

"Here it is," said Nilsson. "It's a bit of a walk."

"Walking'll be good for us," said Fors. "Puts the fat in motion. Maybe we should even do a little bit of jogging?"

Nilsson laughed. "Jogging? The only jogging we do around here is to the pub."

The two men walked next to each other across the empty parking lot.

"Berg claimed that a lot of tourists on the highway would stop here. He built a parking lot for fifty cars. The only time I've seen more than ten cars here is when Berg had a crayfish party at his place."

They turned onto the path. It was a well-groomed gravel trail, two meters wide.

Nilsson pointed. "You see the big rock? That's where I kissed my first girl."

"Really? You're from this area?" Fors said.

"I've lived here my whole life. I was at the police academy in Stockholm, of course. Did two years of service down there. Then I came back up north. There were three of us here then. No cops ever came out from Aln. We would have some trouble in the parks during the summer, drunks at Walpurgis Night and Midsummer's Eve, an ax murder in '67, petty burglaries, otherwise nothing serious. We would just roll up and get out of the car and say 'What's going on here?' That was usually enough. We had a gang of troublemakers here sometime during the sixties. They set up at the campsite— well, now it's the parking lot where we left the car. They stayed there one weekend, drank like you wouldn't believe, and really made a racket. We had a manager at the wood-processing factory back then who had a fourteen-year-old daughter. She liked to do everything her father said she shouldn't. After the hooligans got here, it didn't take two minutes before she joined them. The father called and asked me to bring her home. She was a minor. I took Burman, and we drove up here. Burman was an old-timer. He was as big as a house and as strong as a bear. We went to their campsite. Not a single person was sober, naked girls everywhere. The manager's daughter was named Charlotte. Burman stalked to the middle of the camp and roared, 'It's time to come home, Lotta!' He was holding his baton behind his back. A thin little punk with sideburns came up and threatened him with a beating. 'Threaten me one more time!' Burman suggested. Didn't even blink. I think he was smiling, too. Then the idiot with the sideburns slouched off, and Burman bellowed, 'Lotta, it's time to come home. Now!' And the girl came out of a tent in just her panties. She ran ahead of us to the car. The guy with the sideburns had collected some brave friends. They started heaving bottles at us. It sounds like a funny story after so many years, but let me tell you, I was scared. We got the girl in the car and drove off. It was raining bottles. We had to replace the rear window."

Nilsson paused.

"These days we're more careful. Last month we arrested a boy on Walpurgis Night. He was dead drunk. On his belt he had the kind of knife you use to gut and clean fish—you know, with a thin blade. He had another one in his boot. He said that he had them to defend himself. He was thirteen."

They had made their way along the path to where the river came out of the woods. It was a small river, in some places only a few meters wide and half as deep. The water looked clear.

"They've stocked the river with trout. Berg's idea. He can fish from his backyard."

They continued along the path. The wind pulled at the spruce trees around them. Dry twigs were scattered here and there, torn from the trees on the north side of the path.

"What are we looking for anyway?" Nilsson asked.

"I don't know," Fors replied. "I just wanted to take a look around. The boy went this way. If he met someone who wanted to hurt him, then this seems like a place where they wouldn't be disturbed."

"Definitely," Nilsson said. "There's never anyone here. Except on Saturdays during the summer. Then it's a hangout."

"What kind of hangout?"

"For people who don't have anything better to do. Troublesome kids. But that's during the summer, when it's warm. Berg complains sometimes. He had problems as soon as the road to his house was finished. There were some break-ins. Do you know what he has in his summer house? A wine cellar. They stole twelve bottles of Chablis. I guess he'd planned on drinking them with the trout at some point."

They passed a bench. It was made up of two rough planks attached to cement supports, with another board for the backrest.

"Berg's benches," said Nilsson. "The hooligans usually hang out and drink at the next one down the trail."

They continued walking. Fors asked to borrow Nilsson's cell phone. He dialed a number and got a hold of Söderström, the canine officer. They agreed to meet at the local station between three and four o'clock.

"Have they caught up with the wandering jailbirds?" Nilsson asked when Fors handed back the phone.

"That's what he said."

There were cigarette butts beside the next bench, along with two beer cans glittering on the slope toward the river, which was almost twice as wide here. The sandy bottom shone white. On their side the water wasn't more than a meter high; on the other side it was deeper.

"Do you think something bad has happened to the kid?" Nilsson asked while Fors went and examined the slope going down to the water.

"No idea. What do you think?"

"Another local boy disappeared last summer. He was gone for four days. When he came home, he didn't want to say where he'd been, what he had done, or why he left. He was fifteen."

"Do you know Alf Nordström?"

"Of course. His dad is a guardsman."

"What kind of a guy is he?"

"Sporty type, unmarried. Never had any problems that I know of."

"I need to speak with him one more time. Right now, can you do me a favor? Go back to the car and drive down to the other parking lot I saw on the map where the path comes out. I want to walk the whole trail and get a feel for things. You can meet me."

"Sure," Nilsson said, and turned back for the car.

Fors continued on. After a while he passed a house that he guessed was Berg's summer home. On the other side of the path there was a slightly dilapidated little house painted brown, with roofing tiles covered in brownish yellow pine needles. Fors walked over to it and peered in through the window. The front door and the kitchen door were fortified with large steel bars and heavy hanging locks. The windows weren't broken. Three concrete mushrooms the size of garbage cans were standing in the yard. Fors noted that they were painted to resemble poisonous death caps. The red color on their hats had started peeling.

A man came out of the woods while Fors was peering into the cottage. He was a large, stocky man with a long face.

"What are you doing?" Rake in hand, the man looked threatening.

Fors showed his ID. "And you?" he asked as he pocketed his ID.

"I live here."

"You're Berg?"

"That's right."

"The councilman who calls the shots."

"Is that what they say?"

"That's what I've heard."

"People say a lot of things. I would have liked it if the police had been in touch when I had the break-in a while back. No one even came to take a look."

"Wasn't Nilsson here?"

"Who cares about Nilsson? Someone from the city should have come. Two busloads of police came when they burned a cross in Sållan three years ago. But when ordinary people have a break-in, no one cares."

"What was the story with the cross?"

"You don't remember?"

"I was working in Stockholm at the time."

"Some kids set fire to a cross up by the immigrant housing. There were big headlines in the local papers. The city papers, too. They wrote about us like we were all monsters."

"Wasn't a woman burned?"

"That was an exaggeration. She got a burn on her arm. Look at this; it can happen even when you're burning leaves." Berg held out a hand blotchy where he'd apparently burned himself.

"Don't you want to know what I'm doing here?" Fors asked.

"I already know. You're looking for Eriksson."

"Have you seen him?"

"Not for a long time. I don't even know if I would recognize him."

"Did you know him before?"

"He was a Scout when he was younger. He came up to the council offices one time, but that was several years ago. He was selling newspapers."

"Did you buy one?"

"No."

And while they were talking, Hilmer Eriksson stood next to them. He shouted. He pulled at their arms and pointed to the compost pile in the corner of the dilapidated cottage's yard. But Hilmer was invisible, he couldn't be heard, he wasn't noticed. He was just there, like a powerless witness in the hunt for himself.

His damaged face.

His ruined lips.

Blood on his shirt.

Only one shoe.

"What kind of place is this?" Fors asked.

"What do you mean?" Berg replied, screwing up his eyes as he leaned on his rake.

"How do people make a living?"

"The wood-processing plant and Welux. Welux makes hydraulic systems and brakes. The wood plant will probably have to close soon. We're trying to encourage tourism. It's beautiful in this area. We're focusing on hunting and fishing. Small wild game and trout.

Down on the Continent you're not allowed to eat the fish you catch. Those folks will go crazy when they find out that up here they can catch a pound of trout, make a fire, cook the fish in foil, eat it on a sandwich, and keep fishing. The Germans love that kind of thing. And if they also get to see a moose in the process, then the experience is complete."

"And Sållan?"

"They have some asylum seekers and immigrants up there. It's hard to get the immigrants to work. People grumble. They think it's wrong that these charity cases are so lazy. Unemployment is over sixty percent. We've had our share of problems in Vallen. We had a group of immigrant kids who caused some trouble a few years ago. But it's like that everywhere in this country these days."

Berg paused. "Well, the yard work won't get done if I stand here like this. I've got to go set fire to the leaf pile. I should have done the raking two weeks ago, but you don't have much control over your schedule when you're in politics. Hope you find the boy."

"We'll find him," said Fors. "Don't burn yourself."

Berg walked across the clearing in front of his house, and Fors watched him bend down and light a pile of leaves and branches with a match. Then Fors walked on. Berg was right. The area was beautiful.

After a while he came to a footbridge. It spanned the river right before the waterway was joined by what Fors figured was Flax Creek. The detective left the path, slipped down the bank, and walked out onto a narrow point. The point lay a few meters above the surface of the river. Here, where the two currents met, the water was fairly deep. Fors studied his surroundings but didn't see anything remarkable. He returned to the path and passed the bridge and, after a while, yet another footbridge. Then he came out to a parking lot just as large as the one at the other end of the path. The police car was waiting there.

"Did you find anything?" Nilsson asked when Fors got into the car.

"No. Can you drive me over to Hallby School?"

"If you like," Nilsson said as he put the car in gear and pulled out onto the empty road.

"I met Berg," Fors said after a while. "He was burning leaves."

"People shouldn't be burning when it's this windy," said Nilsson. "We had three forest fires before midsummer last year. None of them spread very far, but almost anything can happen when we have wind like this."

"Maybe he's tired of it all?" said Fors.

"What do you mean?"

"Some people get fed up and decide to ruin things for everyone else."

"Berg isn't like that. He has his bad side, but he's a good man."

Nilsson put on the radio. They were playing an old doo-wop hit.

"Do you remember this one?"

"Yes," said Fors. "I was fifteen the summer it came out. Dad did very well in the chess competition that year. And I bought a Tandberg reel-to-reel tape recorder."

"A Tandberg tape deck," Nilsson mused. "When was the last time you saw one of those around?"

Neither of them said anything else until they got to Hallby School.

"I won't be very long," Fors said when he got out of the car. "You can wait here."

Nilsson nodded, and Fors shut the car door and headed inside.

Hallby School was a three-story brick building. A popular Swedish proverb was etched in stone above the entrance: THE BEST LOAD TO CARRY IS GOOD SENSE.

The heavy door had to be difficult for the younger kids to handle, Fors thought as he pulled it open and stepped inside. His footfalls echoed. He met a whole mass of students in the stairwell. They appeared to be on their way to the lunchroom. He caught a glimpse of women in kerchiefs, white blouses, and aprons, and there was a smell of fried fish.

"The office?" Fors said to a girl with braces.

"Second floor."

He found Nordström in the doorway of a little workroom next to the main office. The janitor was carrying a roll of electrical cord.

"Alf, I need to speak with you again," Fors said.

"Can it wait?"

"No. Now."

Fors followed Nordström into the room. It was little more than a closet, with one window, a small desk with a telephone, and several gray steel file cabinets. A woman stood at the desk, leaning over a schedule. Nordström set the roll of cord on a file cabinet as Fors showed the woman his ID.

"Excuse me, but we're going to need this room for five minutes," he said.

The woman took a stack of books, exchanged a glance with Nordström, and disappeared. Fors closed the door and turned toward the janitor, who was busy with a can of snuff.

"How many students do you have over at Hilmer's school?"

"I've already told you, four parallel tracks per grade. It's just over three hundred students."

"And everyone has his own locker?"

"Of course." Nordström rubbed his chin and returned the can of snuff to his breast pocket.

"How do you keep track of who has which locker?"

"I have a list."

"So you don't know off the top of your head who has which locker?"

"Should I know that?"

"You knew right away which one was Hilmer's."

"Yes."

"Why is that?"

"Some things you just know."

"Do you know who has the lockers next to Hilmer's?"

"I'd need to look that up."

"Why do you know which locker is Hilmer's?"

Nordström sighed. "Is it important?"

"Answer the question."

"I don't know how I know that. Some things you just know."

"It looks like Hilmer's locker has been painted recently."

42 "Oh?"

"Did you recently paint Hilmer's locker?"

"Is this an interrogation?"

"You can call it what you want, but answer the question. You do know if you painted the boy's locker, don't you?"

"I painted it a while ago."

"When?"

"Two weeks ago."

"Why?"

"Because it needed to be painted."

"None of the other lockers near it appear to have been painted recently. Why Hilmer's?"

"I've already told you."

"No, you haven't. Why did you paint his locker?"

Nordström dug the snuff from his mouth with a finger and flicked it in the wastebasket. "Do you have the right to go on like this?"

"I can get you a written summons to come for an interrogation in the city if that's more convenient."

"Someone had vandalized his locker with a marker."

"Who?"

"I don't know."

"What did the graffiti look like?"

"It was a cross."

"What kind of a cross?"

"A swastika."

"How big was it?"

"About fifteen centimeters in diameter."

"What color?"

"Black."

"Was that all?"

"There were three letters there, too."

"Which ones?"

"Three *H*s."

Fors looked around for a piece of paper. There was a stack of photocopier paper on one of the file cabinets. He took a sheet and placed it on the table in front of Nordström. Then Fors removed the ballpoint pen from his inside pocket.

"Draw the swastika in the size at which you saw it."

"I've never been good at drawing."

"We can scrape the paint off the locker if that's easier."

Nordström drew. The swastika covered the entire page. "About like this."

Fors took the paper, folded it twice, and put it in his inside pocket. He placed a new piece of paper in front of Nordström. "The three letters."

Nordström drew the *H*s, which were right next to one another. Fors pocketed that piece of paper, too. "Thanks."

"Are we done now?"

Fors was silent.

"Are we done now?" Nordström repeated.

"Why didn't you tell me this earlier?"

"I didn't think about it."

"What did you do in addition to painting over the graffiti?"

"What do you mean?"

"Didn't you tell the administration that someone had painted a swastika on a boy's locker?"

"Yes."

"Who did you tell?"

"Principal Humbleberg."

"And what did he say?"

"That I should paint over it."

"So it was on Humbleberg's order that you painted the locker?"

"Yes."

"Have you painted over swastikas before?"

"Probably."

"When?"

"A while ago."

"Where?"

"In the locker hall, in the corridor outside the teachers' lounge, on the wall in the gym."

"And who was it who told you to paint them over?"

"Humbleberg."

"When was the first time you painted over a swastika?"

"Several years ago."

"Where was it?"

"The one in the corridor outside the teachers' lounge. Someone had marked little ones on the teachers' mailboxes."

"On all of them?"

"Most of them."

"Was it reported to the police?"

"I don't know. There was damage, so I guess it was reported."

"And then?"

"There was a large swastika on the wall of the gym. It was painted at about the same time as the mailboxes."

"How big?"

"Almost one meter in diameter. High up. Whoever did it must have had a ladder."

"And then in the locker hall?"

"Yes."

"Where?"

"On some lockers."

"Whose?"

"Some of the immigrant kids'."

"When was this?"

"In the fall."

"Thanks. That's everything."

"So I can go now?"

"Yes."

Nordström took his roll of cord and disappeared out the door.

In the parking lot Fors found Nilsson waiting with the car windows open, listening to a radio program about the Faeroe Islands.

"I have some moose steaks at headquarters for lunch," Nilsson said as he turned out of the school's parking lot. "You'd be impressed what I can do with a couple hot plates. Boiled potatoes, lingonberries, and pickles. There's plenty for you."

"That sounds good."

"Did you find out anything?"

"Nordström has spent a lot of time painting over swastikas at Hilmer's school."

"You don't say," Nilsson said, driving stiffly, as if the car were an eighteen-wheeler.

"Do you have a lot of that sort of thing here?"

"Not more than anywhere else."

"Did you investigate any damage at Lugnet School a few years ago?"

"No."

"Are you sure?"

"I've never investigated anything at that school."

"But a swastika had been painted on the wall of the gym?"

"I haven't heard anything about that."

They were quiet for a while.

"What kind of a man is Principal Humbleberg?" Fors asked.

"Farmer's son. Parents still live on the farm. They have woods along the upper reaches of Flax Creek. They've sold the animals. Humbleberg is active in the Center party. A good friend of Berg's, even if they quarrel a bit over politics. Doesn't drink. Did about the same as me, left here for a few years for college. Came back and became a teacher. He's been principal for five or six years. Most people would say he's a good man."

"And you?"

"We go hunting together. He shot a bull moose in the fall. The biggest anyone has seen in ages. We hunt sometimes on his parents' land. Yes, I think he's a good guy."

Nilsson turned into the parking lot next to the town hall. "That's Berg's car," he said, and pointed to a red Volvo when they got out.

Has he already finished burning leaves? Fors wondered.

"Where can the bike be?" he asked.

"The boy's bike? If he ran into trouble on the path, then his bike is probably at the bottom of the river."

Once back inside the station, Nilsson didn't waste time getting the moose steaks started. Fors dialed a phone number. The call was answered almost as soon as he finished dialing.

"Eriksson." It was a soft, tense female voice.

"My name is Detective Harald Fors. I'm handling the police investigation of Hilmer's disappearance. Is this Mrs. Eriksson?"

"Yes. Have you found him?"

"No, we haven't found him. Can I meet with you this afternoon?"

"Of course. When?"

"In about an hour."

"That's fine. I'll be home."

Fors could hear that she was on the verge of tears.

"We're going to find him," he said. "A canine unit is coming up this afternoon. We'll find him."

"That's what Nilsson said," Mrs. Eriksson replied.

"I'll be there in an hour."

The whole time Detective Fors was speaking with Anna Eriksson, Hilmer stood right next to him. Hilmer whimpered and again struggled to remember his mom, his dad, and his sister, Karin, but he couldn't picture them. There was only pain where the images should have been.

The pain of invisibility.

The pain of the tormented body.

The nightmarish pain of powerlessness.

Fors opened his briefcase and took out the notebook. Once again he wrote the day's date and the time and made a note about the walk along the creek and the visit to the school in Hallby.

Then he retrieved the shopping bag and spread out the contents of Hilmer's locker on the desk in front of him. He flipped through the chess book, which he recognized from his father's library. He had read it himself when he was a child and tried to re-create the famous moves.

"Food's ready!" Nilsson yelled from the staff lounge, and Fors went and sat at the table. Nilsson had opened the window. A hard wind was blowing, and it rattled the window frame.

"I'm going to the Erikssons' in a bit," Fors said. "How do I get there?"

"You just continue up the road, past the parking lot by the river trail where we first stopped. It's a yellow house with white eaves and a white fence. Apple trees, flagpole, the whole thing. Let's eat while it's still warm."

Fors cut into his meat. "Did you shoot this yourself?"

"It's a piece of Humbleberg's bull. We always divide the catch. We're a big group, but there was enough for everybody. Pickles?"

For a while they ate in silence, except for the smacking noises made by Nilsson.

Fors decided to pass on a second helping of creamed potatoes.

"More meat?" Nilsson asked when Fors had finished.

"Thanks, but I'm okay."

Nilsson smiled. "It was good I hope."

"Very."

"Come on, have another."

"Once on your lips, forever on your hips," Fors warned.

"You're not a schoolgirl," Nilsson said. "You don't really worry about what ends up on your hips, right?"

"Oh, but I do," Fors objected.

Nilsson laughed. "If I need to reach you, I'll call you on your cell. You can leave your number."

"I left my phone at home this morning," said Fors.

"Then I'll call the Erikssons' if anything comes up. You want coffee?"

"Thanks." Fors got up and closed the window. "Pretty windy."

"It's supposed to get worse," said Nilsson. "A storm like this can take down a lot of trees. How about a pastry for dessert?"

"Hell no."

"I'm joking. You should see the look on your face. Sad to say, I don't have any pastries."

They drank coffee and listened to the wind. Just as Fors set his cup down and was getting ready to make a move, someone came in the main door.

"Anyone here?"

"In the kitchen!" Nilsson hollered.

Olle Berg appeared in the doorway. He did a good job of filling the opening. He looked straight at Fors. "Can I speak with you?"

"Of course."

"Let's step outside."

And Berg led the way out to the municipal parking lot. They ended up beside his red Volvo. The wind was at Berg's back. He turned up the collar on his three-quarter-length jacket.

"I heard that you've spoken with Alf Nordström."

"Yes."

Berg tilted his head and squinted. The wind shifted, and so did the councilman. Dust and grit came swirling up at them. Fors turned his back to the wind and jammed his hands in his jacket pockets.

"This thing with the swastikas is sensitive business," said Berg.

"What do you mean?"

"It can be misunderstood."

"How so?"

"I'm sure you know what I mean."

"No, I don't."

Berg leaned toward Fors. "You don't want this area to get a bad reputation. I'm sure you understand."

Fors sighed. "What do you want, Berg?"

"You don't need to make a mountain out of a molehill, that's all I'm saying."

"Exactly which molehill are you referring to?"

"Don't be an idiot."

"I just don't know what you're talking about."

Berg tried a dejected look. The wind shifted again, and the dust came swirling up from another direction.

"It's only a matter of time before the press plasters this story on the front page. At least in the local papers."

"That Hilmer Eriksson has disappeared?"

"That he's been fighting with the swastika painters."

"I didn't know that," said Fors. "Which boys are they?"

Berg realized that he had said too much. "I don't know exactly who they are, but it's not worth making a big deal out of all the crap boys that age come up with."

"Has Nordström talked to you about any kids that Eriksson might have been fighting with?"

"No."

"Are you sure?"

"Yes. Now I've got to get back. I thought I should talk with you anyway. We're working on making this area into something for tourists from the Continent. We're well on our way."

Berg leaned toward Fors again and drove his hands into his jacket pockets. "You don't think that Fritz and Hans from Berlin will want to come here and fish with their kids if the place gets known as a hangout for Nordic Nazis, do you?"

"Is that what it is?"

Berg shook his head. "Of course not. See you."

Fors watched as the councilman hunkered down against the wind and scuttled toward the front entrance to the municipal building, through which he vanished. Then Fors returned to the station, where Officer Nilsson was doing the dishes.

"I'm leaving now."

"I'll be in touch if there's anything to report," Nilsson replied without turning around.

monday afternoon

detective Fors drove past the river trail parking lot, the wind grabbing and shaking his little car. He slowed down as he approached the yellow house with white eaves. On a blue mailbox, ERIKSSON was painted in careful white lettering. Fors parked in the driveway and got out. A woman with short red hair, wearing jeans and a wool sweater, opened the door and crossed her arms over her chest as if she were freezing. Fors approached. Despite the fact that she was wearing clogs, she barely came up to his chin.

"Harald Fors," he said as they shook hands.

"Anna Eriksson."

She turned and led the way inside. The detective gently pulled the door closed behind him.

The hall was large and bright with white wallpaper, a rag rug on the floor, and some framed photos on the wall.

In one photo, Fors saw a three-year-old girl and a boy about five years older sitting in a small dinghy. Both were laughing.

In another, the same children were on skis a few years later against a backdrop of snow-covered mountains.

Others showed a Norwegian flag against a blue sky, and the same children with dark suntans on what he guessed was a Mediterranean beach.

As was common courtesy, Fors took off his shoes.

Mrs. Eriksson was standing in the doorway to the living room. "Would you like anything?"

"Coffee?"

"I have some here in a thermos."

Fors followed her into the comfortable-looking room. He glanced around. Light-colored furniture, two sofas placed together at an angle, an old tile stove, and a large TV. A great many house-plants. A wall with books from floor to ceiling. Everything in its place, very tidy. Fors walked past the bookshelf toward the tray with coffee.

He sat on a sofa, and Mrs. Eriksson took the recliner across from him. Head lowered, Fors saw that her white clogs were decorated with painted roses.

"I know that you've spoken to Officer Nilsson, but I'd like to talk to you, too, if that's okay."

"Of course. Do you have people searching now?"

"A canine unit is coming this afternoon. The officer is experienced, and he has a good dog."

"Don't you usually use the National Guard to search?"

"We do, when it's a question of smaller children or older people, where the missing person may be disoriented. In this case, it's something we may consider later."

"Why later?" Mrs. Eriksson leaned forward over the tray on the coffee table and took a floral-patterned cup and saucer. Her hand shook as she placed the cup in front of Fors and poured.

"We're shorthanded, and missing teenagers usually show up again on their own after a while. But we're taking this seriously. If Hilmer hasn't come home by tonight, we'll put on as many people as we can."

"Why not do that now?"

"We need to know where to look. That's why I'm here, to try to understand where we should search. I'd like to take it from the beginning. Hilmer was going to get something, is that right?"

"He had come from practice at Vallen. I'd just that day bought two new towels. He'd taken one of them and then left it in the locker room. He said he'd find it at practice on Monday, but I told him he had to go back and get it right away. They were expensive towels."

"Did you exchange words?"

"What do you mean?"

"Did you have a fight?"

"I told him to get the towel, he grumbled a bit, but he left a little while later."

"What time was it then?"

While she was thinking, Fors took his notebook from his briefcase beside him on the sofa. He noted the date, time, and location at the top of a blank page and waited for Mrs. Eriksson to respond. She looked tired, probably hadn't slept well.

"He left between five forty-five and six o'clock."

"Did you look at the clock?"

"Yes, because Hilmer said he wouldn't be back in time for the soccer match on TV, which started at seven. I looked at the clock, and it was only quarter to six, and I knew it wouldn't take more than half an hour for him to bike to Vallen and back. We argued about it for a while. I'm guessing that he left about ten minutes before six."

"And where did he go then?"

"To Vallen, of course."

"Do you know which route he was planning on taking?"

"He probably took the trail."

"Along the river?"

"Yes."

"Did he tell you he was going to go that way?"

"No."

"Did you know that he didn't bike directly to Vallen?"

"What?"

"Hilmer biked to Ellen Stare's house in Vreten first."

Mrs. Eriksson looked surprised. "He went to Ellen's?"

"Yes. But he hadn't said anything to you?"

"Why did he go there?"

"I don't know. What do you think?"

"Ellen was going to go to Stockholm on Saturday. Her grand-mother was turning eighty. They were going to leave sometime in the afternoon."

"Did Hilmer tell you that?"

"I had asked him if Ellen wanted to come here and watch the match. Hilmer told me that Ellen and her mom were going to drive down to Stockholm and wouldn't be home until late Sunday night."

"We know they were still home at six-thirty. Ellen says that Hilmer came to her house around six and left at six-thirty."

"Then he would have been home just in time for the soccer match."

"Is that your guess?"

"Yes."

"He didn't stop by here on his way to Vallen after he had been at Ellen's?"

"No. Why would he do that?"

"I don't know. Do you have a recent photo of Hilmer?"

Mrs. Eriksson got up and went to a set of drawers next to the bookshelf. She opened the top drawer and took out an envelope, from which she slipped some photos. She returned to the coffee table and placed two prints in front of Fors.

"These were taken last winter."

Fors saw a head shot of an ordinary-looking teen—short, light hair, a few pimples, thin lips, serious eyes. The other picture was a full-length shot. Ellen Stare was standing next to Hilmer. Her boyfriend was a bit taller than she was, and Ellen was not what you would call short.

"How tall is Hilmer?"

"Six feet. My husband is six-four."

"When will he be home?"

"He was going to try to come home early. Maybe around three."

"Where does he work?"

"He's a manager at Welux."

"What's his name?"

"Anders."

"And you, where do you work?"

"At a bank in the city. I work part-time."

Fors wrote, and while he was writing, Hilmer sat down on the sheepskin rug next to the tile stove. As a child he had loved lying on the gray wool. Now it was too small for him to lie on, but he lay back anyway. He watched his mother from this odd angle. He was so upset that he had a hard time breathing. Something was bubbling in his throat.

Blood.

Mom.

Then he fell, long and deep down into himself. Away from the pain and into sleep.

Dream.

Fors sipped Mrs. Eriksson's coffee. It was strong but not very warm, and it tasted like a thermos.

"Do you know of any places where Hilmer liked to go when he was younger?"

"What kinds of places?"

"A clubhouse in the woods maybe?"

"Probably."

"Was there a place where he liked to hang out?"

"Not that I know of. He played in the woods, like all of the kids around here." Mrs. Eriksson looked disheartened.

"What kind of bike does Hilmer have?"

"A red mountain bike. Brand-new. I can show you the papers."

Mrs. Eriksson got up and disappeared into the hall. Fors heard her footsteps going up to the second floor. He went to the window and peered out. The lawn was well tended, the apple trees looked as if they had been pruned during the early spring.

Fors thought about the house he had owned in Trollbäcken, south of Stockholm. He thought about the apple trees there that he had pruned. They had never borne fruit.

Mrs. Eriksson came back with a large brown envelope. She held it out to Fors, who returned to the sofa and took out a color brochure, a warranty, and a receipt. The receipt was dated April 12.

"He's so happy with his new bike," Mrs. Eriksson said.

Fors nodded, made a few notes.

"Does Hilmer have any enemies?"

"I don't think so."

"He hasn't told you about any fights or trouble in school?"

"No."

"If he had had a problem of any kind, would he have talked about it?"

"If it was serious. But he's at an age where he wants to be independent."

"Does he have any friends you think he should stay away from?"

"Bad influences?"

"Yes."

"No, I don't think so. He was a Boy Scout for a long time, now he's into soccer and chess. And his computer, of course. He spends a lot of time on his computer."

"Who are his best friends?"

"Ellen is very close to him. They've known each other since grade school and have always gotten along well. They went on a language trip together last summer. But they didn't start dating until the winter. Then there's Daniel. Both of them are in the chess club. He's a good kid."

"Is there anyone in his class who isn't?"

"Well, there's that Henrik Malmsten and Lars-Erik Bulterman. They cause problems for all the kids, not to mention the teachers."

Fors wrote this down. "May I have a look in Hilmer's room?"

"Of course. It's upstairs."

Both of them got up and went into the hall. Fors followed Mrs. Eriksson up the staircase, toting his briefcase and notebook under his right arm.

The room faced south and had a view over the road through the only window. There was a bed and a desk with a computer, two spindle-back chairs, a crowded bookshelf. Two chess books and a chessboard without pieces were lying on the dresser. A few shirts were thrown over one of the chairs. A series of team photos were pinned up above the bed; Hilmer could be recognized in each. Some silver-plated trophies, the size of eggcups, were standing on the windowsill. A pair of soccer cleats had been tossed to the carpet, one lying in the corner by the dresser, the other just by the door.

Mrs. Eriksson looked pained, as if the mess were hers. "He's good at most things, but cleaning isn't one of them."

Fors nodded. "May I look in the drawers?"

"Of course."

The detective walked to the dresser and pulled out the drawers. Underwear, shirts, T-shirts. Nothing special or noteworthy.

Fors went over to the computer. "I'd like to see Hilmer's e-mail, if that's possible."

This request distressed Mrs. Eriksson. "I don't know . . . It's very private. I think he gets a lot from Ellen."

"I understand."

"He also has a password. You can't get into the computer without the password."

Fors nodded and paced over to the window. "Does he get any mail?"

"Regular mail?"

"Yes."

"It's been a long time. Something came from the chess club at Easter. That's all he's gotten recently."

"Who does he talk to on the phone?"

"Ellen, of course. Daniel. Not too many kids. He doesn't have his own phone, so he has to use either the one in the hall or the one in our bedroom."

"How was he dressed when he biked to Ellen's?"

Mrs. Eriksson hesitated, not because she didn't know what Hilmer had been wearing—just the opposite. She hesitated because thinking of the clothes stirred fear—the slow, sucking, worrying fear that is present at every disappearance—the fear that the missing person won't come back.

And then she described her son's pants, shirt, and jacket, down to the stripes on his gym socks.

Fors made careful notes. Out the window he glimpsed a magpie hopping on the lawn.

"I think that's enough for right now. My colleague's name is Officer Söderström. He'll call me in a few hours, before he comes up. May I take this photo?"

"Certainly. But I would like to have it back."

"Of course. May I make a phone call?"

"You can use the phone in the front hall."

She trailed him down the stairs.

"Do you happen to know the number to Hilmer's school?"

In a telephone book with light blue velour covers, Mrs. Eriksson found the listing. She pointed with an unpainted fingernail, and Fors dialed the number.

After speaking to the secretary, he was transferred to Principal Humbleberg. Fors told the principal that he had a few questions and requested an interview in fifteen minutes. The principal said he would be waiting.

Fors then phoned Nilsson at the police station. "I'm going back to Hilmer's school. You can tell Söderström to call me there if he shows up in the next hour."

Fors thanked Mrs. Eriksson for the coffee before he left. The photo of Hilmer was lying next to him on the passenger seat, and the invisible Hilmer himself was in the car as well. The boy's presence was overpowering. Without knowing why, Fors was uneasy and found it difficult to listen to the Mozart piece on the radio.

At the school Fors went right to the rows of lockers. The hall was empty, except for one lone girl. The detective began an examination of each locker door. On one he noted that someone had written a name in a rounded, girlish hand.

KRISTINA GYLLENSTIERNA.

A pair of lightning bolts was scrawled above the name. Fors examined the rest of the lockers in the hall one after the other. Then he went to the office, where he found the principal at his desk. Fors pulled the door shut behind him and sat down across from Humbleberg.

The principal's suit jacket was hanging over the back of his chair. The detective figured that Sven Humbleberg believed a principal should wear a coat and tie to work every day. He took out his notebook, wrote the date and time, and perched the book on Humbleberg's desk, which was still covered with papers and a number of open binders.

Fors cleared his throat. "Stressful job, I've heard, being principal."

"It's not the way it used to be. A lot of administrative work, and you have to know your stuff, otherwise you get your hands smacked by the superintendent. She's a pretty tough cookie."

Fors studied the man on the other side of the desk. He decided they must be about the same age.

"How would you describe this area, Principal Humbleberg?"

Humbleberg didn't respond immediately. He looked as if he was choosing his words carefully.

"It's like a lot of other places around the country. We're plagued by lack of employment opportunities. And this high school is like most schools. There's a small group of kids who learn a great deal, a slightly larger group who don't learn anything at all. And the majority of them get by, absorbing a bit of this and that. The whole thing is a little pointless, like a journey without a destination. I'm supposed to make sure it all goes by the book." With a dejected gesture, Humbleberg leaned back in his chair.

"I've heard that you've had some problems with graffiti."

"We've been blessed with our fair share."

"Blessed?"

"It's a blessing for the people who manufacture paint."

"I don't understand what you mean."

"I don't mean anything in particular. Just that it feels a bit hopeless sometimes."

"But you have Nordström. He says he deals with it."

"That's what I'm saying. We go through a lot of paint."

"Would you describe much of the graffiti as political?"

"That depends on what you mean. These kids aren't exactly what you'd call politically active."

"Who is Kristina Gyllenstierna?"

"Is she supposed to be a student here?"

"Yes."

"We don't have a student by that name."

"Are you sure?"

"Absolutely."

"There's a locker with that name on it."

"The students aren't allowed to write on their lockers, but they do it anyway."

"There's no Kristina Gyllenstierna at this school?"

"No."

"Then I'd like to know who has the locker with 'Kristina Gyllenstierna' written on it."

"That's easy. I'll ask the secretary to look it up."

"Thanks."

Humbleberg leaned forward and pressed the intercom. "Margit, Inspector Fors says there's a locker in the hall with the name Kristina Gyllenstierna written on it. Can you go and see whose it is?" The principal leaned back in his chair again and ran his hand through his hair. "She's checking right now."

"Nordström has painted over a number of swastikas," said Fors.

Humbleberg took a pencil from the desk, twirled it in his fingers, and put it back again.

"Look, there's a lot of nonsense that goes on around here," he said after a while. "Some kids are going to go wrong. We have some rotten eggs at this school. They've learned that they can get an extra rise out of us if they paint a few swastikas here and there. Maybe they do it to vent some frustration with the unemployment situation, who knows? No matter what the decade, kids seem to find some trouble to get into. In my day you could frighten adults by having sex or drinking. These days Mom and Dad give you advice about condoms and STDs after your first time. Parents buy wine for their fifteen-year-olds. Kids always have to find the things that upset us; they have to test the boundaries. That's how I see it."

"What have you done about the graffiti, aside from painting it over?"

"We've tried to identify the culprits. We have our theories, but sometimes theories are hard to prove."

"So what are you doing about it?"

Humbleberg threw his arms wide. "What would you have done?"

"I don't know. But I'm not the principal here. It's not my job to know what to do when kids are painting swastikas in my school."

Humbleberg played with the pencil again. "I'm going to tell you what I think. I think the less attention you give these bad seeds, the better."

"That's what you think?"

"Yes."

Fors took notes. "So what did you do?"

"When we started finding swastikas? I told you. We tried to figure out who the vandals were. I spoke with the teachers and asked them to discuss it in their classes."

"What do you mean by 'it'?"

"Nazi symbols, slogans, and everything they represent."

"Did the teachers do what you asked?"

"I assume so."

"When was the first swastika painted at the school?"

Humbleberg thought. "It was five years ago. On the wall of the gymnasium."

"Nordström said the culprit had to have used a ladder."

"That's right."

"And after that you spoke with the teachers, and they spoke with the students, but then there were more swastikas?"

"Yes. After a few months, the hall outside the school office was vandalized."

"That's where the teachers' mailboxes are?"

"Yes."

"It was reported to the police, right?"

"I actually don't recall."

"My colleague Nilsson says that he doesn't remember any investigation of vandalism at the school."

"It's possible that we didn't report it."

As Fors made notes, there was a knock at the door.

The secretary poked her head in. "The locker belongs to Anneli Tullgren."

"Thanks, Margit," said Humbleberg.

"Anneli Tullgren," Fors repeated as he wrote down the name. "What class is she in?"

"9C."

"Can you bring her here?"

"Of course, if she's at school today." Humbleberg leaned forward over the intercom again. "Margit, can you ask Anneli in 9C to come here?"

Then he got up and put on his suit jacket. He apparently felt he needed to explain why. "I think I'm coming down with something. A cold, I feel a bit chilled." He watched Fors, still leaning over his notes. "Tell me, what does all this have to do with the disappearance of Hilmer Eriksson?"

And neither of them saw Hilmer.

Bleeding on the floor.

Mouth stuffed full.

Rotting wet leaves.

On the floor, right in front of them.

• • •

"I don't know," said Fors. "What do you think?"

Humbleberg seemed startled. "What do you mean?"

"What do *you* think?"

"About what?"

"You know Councilman Berg, don't you?"

"Of course."

"Both of you are involved in local politics, right?"

"But not in the same party."

"No, but you know each other rather well?"

"Yes."

"Berg says that Hilmer Eriksson has been fighting with some
boys who painted swastikas."

"Really? I didn't know that."

"Isn't it strange that he knows more than you do?"

"No. Nordström is involved with the local council. Berg probably
knows everything that Nordström knows. They're in the same
party."

"So Nordström knows things you don't?"

"A principal doesn't know everything."

"But if one of your students has been fighting with some neo-
Nazi types here at school, shouldn't you as principal know about
it?"

Humbleberg shook his head. "We don't have any neo-Nazis here.
We have some troublemakers who do what they can to scare us
adults. No one gets anywhere by calling them neo-Nazis."

"Who are these troublemakers you're talking about?"

Humbleberg paused for a moment. "Since I don't have enough
information about any particular incident, it seems wrong to single
anyone out. If I had something more concrete, it would be easier."

"Swastikas aren't concrete?"

"Yes, but even if I think I know who painted them, there's still
an enormous difference between believing and knowing. And if I

start labeling kids as neo-Nazis based on a few tussles they've had with other students, things will go to hell in a hurry. We have squabbles between kids all the time, that's part of the game, but I would never call it criminal activity."

While Fors made careful notes, Humbleberg took a call and said that he was busy for the next half hour. When he hung up the phone, there was a knock at the door and Margit reappeared.

"Here's Anneli."

A tall girl was standing behind the secretary. She had light hair pulled into a ponytail, a face free of makeup, and thin lips. Wide hipped and a bit overweight, she was wearing black boots, baggy black pants, and a gray shirt.

Margit closed the door, and Humbleberg cleared his throat. "Detective Fors here is a police officer. I think he'd like to ask you some questions." Then the principal turned toward Fors. "I assume you'd like to be alone?"

"Not at all," Fors replied. "Please sit down."

The girl took a few steps across the room and sat down in the empty chair in front of Humbleberg's desk. Fors flipped to a clean page in his notebook, wrote the date, then looked at the clock and recorded the time.

"As the principal said, my name is Fors. I'm a police officer, and I'd like to ask you some questions. How do you spell your name?"

Anneli spelled it out.

"Could you write it here for me?" Fors asked as he turned to a new page and held out the notebook and pen. She wrote her name. The handwriting was curvy and girlish. The detective retrieved his notebook and pen.

"So your name is Anneli?"

The girl gave a smile that edged close to a sneer. "You think I'm lying? I just wrote it down for you."

"But there's another name on your locker?"

"Yes."

"What name is on your locker?"

"Kristina Gyllenstierna."

Fors held out the notebook again. "Could you write that as well on the same page?"

"Of course." And Anneli wrote it out.

Fors took his notebook back and looked at the two names. "Are you the one who wrote 'Kristina Gyllenstierna' on your locker?"

With another smile Anneli looked from Fors to Humbleberg and then to Fors again. "What is this? An interrogation?"

"This is not an interrogation," said Fors. "An interrogation would mean that you are suspected of doing something criminal. You may have written 'Kristina Gyllenstierna' on your locker, which possibly breaks a school rule, but it is hardly a criminal act that would result in a police investigation."

Fors waited a moment before he continued. "Aren't you the one who wrote 'Kristina Gyllenstierna' on your locker?"

"Yes, I am," Anneli said, and smiled wide. "Can I go now? I'm missing math. It's my favorite subject."

"Just a little longer," said Fors. "Someone marked two lightning bolts over the name on your locker."

Anneli turned serious. "What about it?"

"Did you do the lightning bolts as well?"

"I won't answer that."

"Why not?"

Anneli didn't respond.

Fors waited.

Humbleberg was quiet.

The sound of shouting children filtered through the closed windows. Kids were out on the playground.

• • •

Hilmer lay on the floor of the office, curled up in pain, sobbing. He wished that he could leave the room on his own, but it was no longer possible. He had hardly any strength left; his only chance was to follow Fors.

"Can I go back now?"

"I'd like to ask a few more questions," said Fors.

"But I don't want to answer," Anneli said. She got up, went for the door with quick steps, and closed it without a sound.

Humbleberg sighed. "She's a bright girl but a bit lost. What did you say is on her locker?"

"Double lightning bolts, Principal. Just like the insignia of Hitler's SS troops. Who are her friends?"

"Bulterman and Malmsten in 9A. They're our troublemakers."

"Tullgren, Bulterman, and Malmsten," said Fors. "Are they the ones painting swastikas?"

Humbleberg shook his head. "I can't prove anything. But I'd guess that each of them has a finger in the paint bucket."

"What kinds of kids are they?"

"Henrik Malmsten isn't the sharpest tool in the shed, but he comes from a pretty good family. His father has a locksmith shop in town. I know his mother from the church choir. Lars-Erik Bulterman has it worse. His mom is a drunk, and his father lost his job a few years ago when Welux was purchased by a group of companies based in Dublin. They cut more than half their employees here. The father has a reputation for being difficult, and it causes problems for him. Like father, like son. Both are aggressive, hot tempered. Bulterman is no idiot, but when it comes to schoolwork, he lacks motivation."

"I'd like to meet Henrik Malmsten. Can you ask him to come here?"

Humbleberg used his intercom to send Margit on the errand. Then he leaned back and sneezed three times, mopping his nose with a handkerchief.

"What can you do?" The principal sighed, disconsolate. "We used to have a good support network for the students. Psychologist, social worker, school counselor. We had a great counselor. We even had several special-education teachers. We would have regular conferences about the students. Most of that is gone now. These days every bit of funding is a struggle, and the school system is all about grades and test results. The teachers are becoming gray-haired burnouts. I'm one of the youngest among the staff. I don't blame anybody. It's just too hard. I have some teachers here that I really feel sorry for. The last thing we needed was the swastikas."

"When did you say the first one was painted?"

"Five years ago."

"It hardly seems possible that Bulterman and Malmsten painted it. Didn't they attend another school back then?"

"They went to the middle school down the road. No, it couldn't have been Bulterman and Malmsten that time."

"So who was it?"

Humbleberg sneezed again with the handkerchief over his mouth.

Fors waited for an answer.

"You'll probably hear it from someone else if I don't say anything, so I may as well tell you myself." The principal's eyes wandered toward the window.

"It's quite windy," said Fors.

More silence. Humbleberg lowered his voice when he started speaking again. "You've met Margit Lundkvist, the one working in the office."

Fors nodded.

"We lived together. Separated last year, after eight years. I don't have any kids of my own, but Margit has a son, Marcus. He's twenty-one now. He was thirteen when Margit and I began living together. I became a sort of father figure for him. He was still a good kid at thirteen. Around the age of fifteen, something went wrong. I never understood what it was that happened. One day he came home wearing a shirt with a swastika on it. I reasoned with him. I tried to make him see why it was so offensive. He was a smart kid, always liked to ask questions. It was usually easy for us to talk. But not this time. He had read much more about the subject than I ever had. He hit me with names and dates. He questioned what I was saying. He refused to take off the shirt."

Humbleberg twirled a pen from the desk. "His taste in music changed. Instead of girls and sex and love, the music was filled with hate."

Humbleberg sighed. "He had new friends, older kids, from Aln. They had shaved heads, black clothes, and they were scary as hell. They'd sit in his room and play that awful skinhead music. I really was scared. He was only in ninth grade when the big swastika in the gym was painted. It was in the fall, school had just started. As far as I know, he was the only skinhead enrolled in the school at that time. He saw his new friends on weekends. When it was warm they all hung out on the river trail, which had just been finished. They drank beer, made noise, and scared people who happened to pass by. Marcus really admired those kids.

"I don't have proof, but I'm almost certain that Marcus was the one who painted the swastika on the gym wall. I think he was the one who vandalized the teachers' mailboxes, too. Whoever did the vandalizing seemed to have gotten in with a key. But I didn't have the energy to follow through. I didn't even report it to the police. I wanted to protect Margit. She's had a hard time, harder than anyone can imagine. No one can understand what a boy like that does to his mother unless they've seen it themselves. Endless sleepless nights. Guilt and the feeling of having failed, of not being good enough. It's terrible."

Humbleberg was silent for a while.

"I wouldn't mention Marcus if I didn't seriously think he could be involved. Whoever painted the swastika on Hilmer's locker also painted the three *H*s. Marcus has spoken a lot about those *H*s."

"What do the three *H*s mean?" asked Fors.

"Hate. Harass. Hero."

Fors wrote for a while, then he looked up. Humbleberg had set his elbows on the desk and was leaning forward.

"Where is Marcus?"

"He lives in the city."

"Does he have contact with Bulterman and Malmsten?"

"I've seen them together. But mainly he's had contact with Anneli Tullgren."

"Really? How so?"

"She's his girlfriend."

"How do you know that?"

"He told me."

There was a knock at the door, and Margit peeped in. Fors looked up, and she quickly met his gaze. "Henrik hasn't been in school since lunch. He seems to have gone home."

"Thanks," Humbleberg said, and Margit closed the door.

Fors pocketed his pen and gathered his things. "May I use the telephone?"

"Go right ahead."

Fors called Nilsson. "Have you heard from Söderström?"

Nilsson said no.

"Do you know a boy named Henrik Malmsten?"

"Yes."

"He left school around lunch. Do you think you can find him?"

"It shouldn't be a problem unless he's gone to the city."

"Pick him up, and call me when you've got him. I'll be at the school a little while longer."

When Fors had set down the receiver, the intercom beeped.

Margit's voice came through. "Blad from the real estate office would like to speak with you, Sven. He's in the teachers' lounge. What should I do?"

The principal looked at Fors. "I have a meeting."

"You've given me a lot of information. Thanks. May I use your telephone for a little while?"

"Of course."

"I need to call Stockholm. How do I get on a line where I can make a long-distance call?"

The principal showed him how, then left for his meeting, taking one of the binders from his desk.

Fors dialed the number of the Criminal Intelligence Service at the National Police Headquarters in Stockholm. A woman with a drawling voice and a southern Swedish accent answered.

"Almgren, CIS."

"My name is Detective Harald Fors. Is Levander there?"

"I'll check. One second."

Fors tried to remember who Almgren could be, but the name didn't ring any bells.

The woman's voice returned. "What was your name again?"

"Harald Fors."

It became quiet again. Then a man's voice could be heard. "Levander."

"Hi, Göran, it's Harald."

"Well, well. So you're not out mushroom picking or whatever it is you do up there in the woods?"

"Not exactly."

"You don't miss Stockholm?"

"Sometimes."

"We miss you."

"It's mutual. Can you help with something?"

"Maybe."

"Who is Kristina Gyllenstierna?"

It took a while for Levander to answer. "She lived at the beginning of the fifteen hundreds, was married to Sten Sture, and played a political role in the battle against the Danes. She supposedly led the charge in defending Stockholm against King Christian; he's the one we call Christian the Tyrant, but to the Danes he's the hero king. Where did you come across her?"

"At a school where I'm doing an investigation. The name's written on a student locker. The double lightning bolt insignia, too."

"Then you've stumbled into a wasps' nest. Kristina Gyllenstierna is also the name of a Nazi women's organization. It was formed during the twenties by a number of upper-class Swedish women. The organization occasionally fades away but then comes roaring back again. At the moment it's alive and well and busy recruiting converts. New blood for the Nazi cause. And the girls aren't just cheerleaders. They're as vicious as the boys. You'd be blown away to see how brutal some of those girls can be."

"Thanks," said Fors.

"If you learn anything about Gyllenstierna, you can write a report. I promise to classify it so that we can find it with at least ten different search words."

"I'll think about it."

"Do that. Are you coming to Stockholm?"

"Probably not before the summer."

"How is your boy doing?"

"He turned thirteen not too long ago. He wanted an iPod. He got a sports watch. Does that make me a bad father?"

"Not at all. Listen, I've got a meeting. The new boss doesn't tolerate tardiness. He calls his leadership style 'management by terror.' He says he learned it at a course where the national police commissioner ended up in tears."

After hanging up, Fors took his briefcase and went back to the locker hall. Classes had just ended for the day, and the hall was filled with students. Fors found Ellen Stare at one of the lockers, putting on her coat.

"Could I speak with you for a few more minutes?"

"You haven't found Hilmer?"

"No. Can we go outside?"

She nodded, closed her locker, and grabbed her school bag as Fors led the way down the hall and out the doors. The breeze was just as stiff as it had been earlier.

75

Ellen squinted. "I'll be riding home against the wind."

"On your bike?"

"Yes."

"Has Hilmer ever said anything to you about being threatened?"

"No."

"Are you sure?"

Ellen seemed to hesitate as Fors held his briefcase against his chest and waited.

"He was in a fight a month ago."

"With who?"

"There's a girl in 9C. Her name is Anneli."

"I've met her."

"Hilmer got in the middle of a fight she was having with a boy in the seventh grade."

"Which boy?"

"His name is Mahmud."

"What did Hilmer tell you?"

"That he was just going to his locker one day and caught Anneli beating up Mahmud. She had him on the floor and was kicking the crap out of him. Hilmer told her to stop. She got furious and started in on Hilmer. He held her off, but then Bulterman showed up and got involved. There was almost a huge fight, but then Nordström, the janitor, broke it up."

"When did this happen?"

"About a month ago."

"Did you see what they wrote on Hilmer's locker?"

"It says 'traitor' now. Before, there was a swastika and other stuff. But Nordström painted over that."

"Do you know who wrote 'traitor'?"

"I can take a guess."

"But you don't know for sure?"

"No."

"Who would you guess it was?"

"Bulterman or Malmsten. They've done almost all of the graffiti in the school."

"This girl, Anneli, do you know her?"

"No, but everyone's afraid of her. She's crazy."

"How so?"

"She loves to fight. She doesn't just get into fights. She makes sure she gets into fights. Hitting people is her hobby."

"Who has she fought?"

"I think there are three or four kids in her class who are afraid to go to school because of her. Everyone knows that she's with Marcus, and no one wants him coming after them. You don't mess with Anneli, it's just the way it is."

"But Hilmer did?"

"He would never stand there and let someone do what she was doing. He'd get involved. That's the way he is."

"I see."

"Are you going to find him?"

"Absolutely."

"Do you think he's run into someone . . . someone who hurt him?"

"I don't know. At this point I'm just asking questions. Thanks for your help. I hope the wind doesn't slow you down too much."

She gave Fors a careful smile and walked away. The detective returned to the school building. He went up to the office and knocked on the secretary's door.

"Do you have some time for me, Margit?"

She turned around and stood up from the computer. Her chair was the same kind Alf Nordström had in his office. "I'll be done in just a minute. Can you wait?"

"Sure. I'll be in the teachers' lounge," said Fors.

Margit nodded and turned back to her work.

In the lounge, Fors had his pick of three sofas. The furniture looked new. Framed photographs of students and teachers on school field trips decorated the walls. Fors recognized Humbleberg in one of the photos. He was wearing cutoff shorts, and he had a beard. He was standing on a beach with a girl in braces in front of a canoe. It looked like early summer. The faded photo seemed about ten years old.

Fors had barely sat down when Margit appeared in the doorway. "Officer Nilsson is on the phone for you. You can take it in the principal's office."

His colleague had good news. "Malmsten is sitting in the kitchen here eating a pastry. I've told him that you're on your way," said Nilsson.

"Good. Give the boy another pastry and tell him that we're getting nowhere looking for Hilmer up by the river. We're hoping Henrik can give us a tip. And for God's sake don't be threatening. Say that we need help, nothing else. I'm coming right away. There's something I want to try."

"Got it," Nilsson said, and hung up.

Fors found Margit. "Can we meet tonight instead?"

"That's fine," the secretary answered. "I'll be home."

"I'll be in touch," Fors said, and then he walked with quick steps through the hall with the lockers and across the school yard to his car. It took less than five minutes to drive to the station.

He found Henrik Malmsten still sitting at the staff-lounge table. Nilsson was tidying the mugs and glassware in the cupboard over the counter. He was in his shirtsleeves, with his back turned to Fors and the boy.

"Henrik is a good kid," said Nilsson as he worked. "He's going to join the guard. We need more guys like him who aren't afraid to get their hands dirty."

"You saw me this morning, right?" Fors said, and sat down across from Henrik Malmsten.

"Yes."

"For a while we thought that Hilmer had been on the river trail on Saturday, but now we figure he must have been somewhere else. We finished searching up there and are going to start looking in Sållan. You were hanging out on the trail on Saturday. Did you see Hilmer?"

"No," Henrik replied.

"That's what I thought," said Fors. "When did you get there?"

Henrik looked uncertain.

"About what time?"

"I don't know."

"But if you guessed?"

"Around five, maybe."

"And when did you leave?"

"Don't know."

"Was it dark?"

"No."

"And you didn't see Hilmer?"

"No."

"Are you sure?"

"Yes."

"What if you went into the woods to take a leak or something? Could Hilmer have passed by while you were gone?"

Henrik smiled. "I pissed by the bench."

"Was it the first or the second bench on the trail?"

"The one by the big house."

"Berg's house?"

"Yes."

"Are you sure that your friends didn't see anyone?"

"I didn't see anyone. They couldn't have seen anyone either."

"That was Lars-Erik and Anneli?"

"Maybe."

"You're helping us, Henrik. We know we've searched the wrong place. If you three were sitting on a bench by the river the whole night, Hilmer could hardly have biked by without you noticing, right?"

Henrik didn't reply.

"Right?" Fors repeated.

Nothing.

"Right?" Fors said a third time.

"I don't know," said Henrik. "I don't even know if we were there."

"No? Then where were you?"

Henrik stared at the table for a moment. "I gotta go home now. Mom's waiting. Dad, too. I need to help them with something."

"Of course," said Fors. "Thanks for your time. Just one more question. Do you think that Hilmer can be up in Sållan? That something happened to him up there?"

Henrik shrugged his shoulders.

"Possibly?"

Henrik was quiet.

"Never mind. You've helped us a lot," Fors said, and held out his hand.

The boy grasped it, smiling uncertainly.

"I told you he's a good kid," said Nilsson. "Take it easy, Henrik."

The boy said goodbye, and then he walked out of the room. The policemen listened for the front door to close behind him.

Nilsson watched Fors. On the tabletop, the detective drummed his briefcase with his fingers. Then, after fidgeting with the bronze zipper tab for a moment, he went to the telephone.

He called Hammarlund at his office in the city. "Listen, Chief. We have a boy who is probably lying in the woods up here, probably assaulted. I want as many people as you can spare. I want Stenberg and Johansson, and I want at least one dog, and I need it now."

Fors heard the sound of shuffling papers. "But you've got Söderström."

"He hasn't come."

"Are you sure?"

"It's just a guess, but I'd be shocked if I were wrong. Also, it'll be dark soon, so we'll need lights."

"I'll see what I can do."

Fors was still holding the phone when Tom Söderström came into the station. A large German shepherd was on a lead at his side. The dog was named Joop and had a reputation for finding missing persons, young or old. Joop was also known for being quick with his teeth if he needed to protect his master.

"Can we start right away?" Söderström asked as soon as he saw Fors. "My sister is visiting. She's leaving tomorrow for home. I've hardly had a chance to talk with her, and she's come all this way just to see me."

"Chief, Söderström is here now," Fors said into the phone, but Hammarlund had already hung up.

"We can get started, can't we?" Söderström asked.

"Of course," said Fors. "Take Nilsson with you. He can show you around. I'll come by soon."

As they were all getting ready to go, Hammarlund called back for Fors.

"You'll get Stenberg and Johansson and two more guys. I don't know which ones yet. Ask Söderström to call when he comes."

"He's here now. Nilsson can tell you where the others should meet them."

Twenty minutes later, Fors pulled up outside Margit Lundkvist's small home. He had tried to catch her at the school, but she had left for the day.

Margit's house reminded Fors of the house in which his ex-wife had grown up in the suburbs outside Stockholm. Compact and practical, it was built in a style that became popular in Sweden in the late 1940s. Fors knew the layout: two small bedrooms, eat-in kitchen, living room.

Fors parked right in front of the gate, black ironwork with a flower pattern. He didn't bother locking the car. Just inside the small yard, a blue woman's bicycle leaned against the fence. A flagpole stood in front of the house. No flag flew, but the halyard whipped against the pole in the stiff wind.

Fors made his way to the door, which was pulled open almost the moment he rang the bell, as if Margit had been waiting for him on the other side.

"The wind is just terrible" was the first thing she said. With an effort, she pushed the door shut behind him. "I've just got dinner started, could you wait a minute?"

Fors nodded. He stood next to the hall rack, which held some hangers, two jackets, and a raincoat. Appetizing smells drifted from the kitchen, but the detective couldn't tell what she was cooking.

"Please, make yourself at home!" Margit called.

As Fors walked toward the living room, he passed the kitchen doorway and glimpsed Margit on her knees, tending to a dish in the oven. The living room was neat as a pin but crowded with furnishings, including a red plush recliner and a bulky hardwood coffee table. The decor was typical: beige carpet with rust brown squares, white curtains, geraniums, a souvenir shelf with glass animals, a cuckoo clock on the wall behind the sofa, a crocheted cloth atop the TV. A fireplace with three decorative birch logs looked clean and unused. In front of a window, Fors noted a gateleg mahogany dining table and three straight-back chairs lined against the wall next to it. A stack of newspapers lay atop the table, precisely parallel to one of the sides. Fors looked at the cuckoo clock long enough to see it wasn't working.

"Would you like anything?" Margit asked, bustling in to stand behind him.

"No thanks. Could we sit down?"

"Of course. Please."

Margit walked past Fors and settled herself at one side of the sofa. Fors chose the red recliner. The armrests were worn. From his ever-present briefcase he took out the notebook, looked at his wristwatch, and wrote the time.

"Margit *Lundkvist*," he said. "Correct?"

He had seen the name on the door to her office at the school, and Humbleberg had mentioned it, but it was a good way to start the conversation.

"Yes."

"Do you spell it with a *k* or a *q*?"

"With a *k*."

"How long have you worked at the high school?"

"Fifteen years."

"You know all of the students?"

"Most of them."

"You have a son who attended the school?"

"Yes. Marcus."

"How old is he?"

"Twenty-one."

"Where does he live?"

Margit had her hands resting in her lap. Now she started scratching the top of her left hand with the nails of her right. The nails were unpainted and had clearly been chewed.

"May I ask something?" she said.

"Of course."

"What is the point of all this?"

"This conversation?"

"Yes."

"I'm investigating the disappearance of Hilmer Eriksson."

"And that's why you want to know where Marcus lives?"

"Yes."

"May I ask why?"

"Because Marcus might know something about where Hilmer is."

Margit took a deep breath and lifted her hands from her lap. "But why would he know something about Hilmer?"

"I don't know. What do you think? Do you think he knows anything about Hilmer?"

Margit was silent.

Is she wondering what there is to know about the one who has disappeared?

What there is to know about the person who has become invisible?

What there is to know about the person who lies bleeding, whose mouth is stuffed with rotting, wet leaves?

"Sven Humbleberg told me about Marcus's troubles and that he's been seeing Anneli Tullgren."

"Yes. But what does that have to do with Hilmer?"

"I don't know if it has anything to do with Hilmer, but it seems to be worth investigating. Based on what I understand, Anneli Tullgren and Hilmer had some kind of dispute a month ago."

"I don't know anything about that."

"Where does Marcus live?"

Margit sighed and mentioned an address in the city.

"Has he lived there long?"

"Since he moved out in the fall."

"Where does he work?"

"He's unemployed."

"Is Marcus here often?"

"He comes home sometimes. He still has things in the basement."

"When was he here last?"

"It's been a while."

"An estimate."

"I think he was out here on Saturday, but he didn't stop by."

"How do you know he was here?"

"He said so. He'd told me he was coming by to get some things, but then he never did. I called in the evening, and he said that he'd been around but hadn't had time to stop by the house."

"Do you know what he was doing here?"

"No."

"Does he come by bus?"

"He has a car."

"How can he afford a car if he's unemployed?"

Margit didn't answer.

"Were you the one who paid for it?"

"Yes."

"And how much did the car cost?"

"A lot."

"Your savings?"

"Yes."

"Kids are expensive."

"In more ways than one."

"What do you mean?"

"I never thought it would be like this."

"How is it?"

"A son who only hates."

"Is that all he does?"

"That's all he ever talks about."

"Who does he hate?"

"Everyone." She rubbed the palms of her hands against her thighs, giving him a gaze that asked him to tell her that it wasn't her fault, that there was something wrong inside Marcus's head.

"You're disappointed?"

She shook her head and went back to scratching her hand. "*Disappointed* isn't the right word. The last five years have been . . . hell, plain and simple."

"What exactly has happened?"

She sighed deeply, her eyes filling with tears. "He was fifteen when it started. Well, I assume Sven told you some of it. I would never have had the strength if it hadn't been for Sven. I would have walked away from all of it."

"How did it start?"

"New, older friends, his room filled with flags, pamphlets, and military gear—old medals and knives."

"Bayonets?"

"With those crosses on them."

"Swastikas?"

"Yes. And the terrible music. Around the clock."

She leaned back and dried her cheeks with the palms of her hands.

"Marcus's father?" Fors asked.

"They've never met."

"Why not?"

She slowly shook her head. "It's a long story. Sometimes, especially at night, you wonder about the mistakes you've made, you think that if you could live your life over, you'd do everything differently."

"What is his name?"

"Marcus's dad? Hans."

"He doesn't live here?"

"He lives in Stockholm."

"And Marcus has never seen his father?"

"We separated when Marcus was six months old. I moved home again. We haven't had any contact in almost twenty years."

"He hasn't been in touch?"

"One time, when Marcus turned three. He sent a picture book. That's it."

"They don't see each other?"

She slowly moved her head to one side, as if she didn't want to indicate a clear no.

Fors took notes to the sound of the halyard slapping against the flagpole outside.

"I'm going to fix that," he said without looking up. "When I leave."

"What?"

"The line on the flagpole. I'll wind it around the pole a few times and pull it tight. It will stop making a noise then."

"Oh, sorry. I didn't realize it was bothering you."

Suddenly, Fors noticed he was still wearing his shoes. He had taken them off at the Erikssons', but here he had forgotten. He scolded himself. *You tiptoe respectfully at the victim's home but not around the possible culprit's mother. Do you think one of these two mothers is less a victim than the other?*

"Excuse me?" said Margit as Fors muttered.

"It's nothing . . . How long have Marcus and Anneli been together?"

"Since the fall."

"Do you know Anneli?"

"I know who she is."

"But do you know her?"

"She's a girl people talk about almost every day. There are teachers in the school who are threatening to take sick leave if she sticks around."

"She's difficult?"

"Some people think she's impossible."

"Where does she live?"

Margit pointed. "Next street over, the house with the Mexican-style brick. Her mother, Berit, owns the convenience store next to the bus station. Her stepfather used to be a truck driver."

"Do you know them?"

"I shop in the store. You hear things."

"What things?"

"Berit had some break-ins a few years ago. One after the other. I think there were four in a row. Her husband hid in the store one Saturday night and waited. The thieves were two immigrants from Sållan. Anneli's stepfather ambushed them. He hit one with an iron rod and broke his collarbone. There was a trial. The step-father got six months in jail. The burglars got only a fine and probation. I think that's what got Anneli's hate fired up. It started at home."

"When did you say this happened?"

"It must have been four years ago."

"But before that? What was Anneli like?"

"She's always been difficult. Before this thing with the break-ins, it was like there was something wrong with everything and everyone. Then it became focused in one direction."

"In what direction?"

"The immigrants."

"So Anneli is known for her beliefs?"

"Yes."

"And now Marcus and Anneli are together?"

"Yes."

"They have this hatred in common?"

"Most likely that's what keeps them together."

"Has Marcus ever said anything about Hilmer?"

"Never."

"Are you sure?"

"He's never said a word about Hilmer. Hilmer is so much younger, they don't hang out. Anyway, Marcus doesn't talk with me so much anymore."

Margit pointed at the cloth on top of the TV.

"I used to have his photo there. But I put it away a while ago. I can't stand to look at it. It's gone that far."

"May I see the photo?"

Margit got up, went to the mahogany table, and pulled out a drawer. She took out a large picture. It was in a gray frame. The picture showed a boy about twelve years old, standing in front of the ocean. He looked straight into the camera and held a fishing pole in his hand. It was summer, and the boy was suntanned and smiling.

Fors looked at the picture for a while before he handed it back. Margit returned it to the drawer. She remained standing by the table, looking out through the window.

"I'm worried about that pine tree," she said. "If it falls this way, it will come down right over the roof."

She was quiet for a while. Then she continued. "People always blame everything on the single mom. If only she hadn't gotten divorced, they say. If only the boy had had a real father, he wouldn't have lost his way. But there are lots of boys who grow up without a father. Only a few go bad. It can't be just because they don't have a father. What do you think?" She looked expectantly at Fors.

"I don't know," he answered.

"But what do you think?"

She was desperate to be freed from her guilt.

"I really don't know," said Fors. He could only investigate, not liberate.

The liberator was someone else.

And the whole time they were speaking, Hilmer glided around the room. He moved silently along the walls; he was right there with them like odorless smoke.

He was the one who was missing.

He searched.

He whispered her name.

He cried her name.

Ellen.

• • •

Fors returned the notebook to his briefcase. "Thanks for your help," he said.

"What help?"

"I'm trying to figure out where we should search. You've been helpful."

Margit tested the soil of a houseplant with a finger. "Marcus was one of the reasons Sven and I split up. For a time, Sven was chairman of the local council. Having a skinhead for a stepson was a problem. Mind you, it hasn't been great for me either. All it's brought me is worry and tears. Nights are the worst."

Fors got up, and she followed him to the door.

"I hope you find him," she said.

"We'll find him," said Fors. "Now I'll take care of that line for the flag."

In the concrete base of the flagpole, someone had marked a date: JUNE 12, 1957. At that time Fors had just finished his final year in middle school. He remembered that at graduation his mother wore a blue polka-dot dress and that he had given the teacher flowers. While he wound the halyard around the pole and secured it, he tried to but couldn't recall what kinds of flowers they had been.

Fors had just opened his car door when a light blue Opel pulled to a stop behind his VW. The sun visor on the passenger side was folded down so that a handwritten sign was visible through the windshield.

PRESS.

The woman behind the wheel had stopped her car millimeters behind the VW, and now she got out. She wore jeans and a denim jacket over a high-necked pink angora sweater. She was short and had light blond hair, which stood up in two pigtailed tufts. Fors figured her to be about thirty.

She introduced herself as Annika Båge, a reporter for the area paper. As they shook hands, Fors introduced himself.

"You're looking for Hilmer Eriksson?"

"Yes."

"How is it going, Detective?"

"We're looking."

"Can you tell me anything about the search?"

"It's too early."

"Are there many people involved?"

As the questions flew, Båge had slipped a small spiral notepad and a pen out of the breast pocket of her jean jacket and was scribbling away.

"There are a few of us."

"Do you suspect foul play?"

"At this stage we know that Hilmer disappeared around six-thirty on Saturday evening. No one has seen him since."

The reporter pointed with her notepad at the house with the flagpole.

"Does your visit to Margit Lundkvist have anything to do with the investigation?"

"Margit works at Hilmer's high school in Lugnet and knows most of the students. She's helping us find out more about them."

"Which students are you trying to find out about?"

"I can't comment on that."

"She has a son who is known for his neo-Nazi sympathies. Does your visit at Margit's have anything to do with him?"

"No comment."

"When are you going to find Hilmer Eriksson?"

"I don't know."

"What do you think happened?"

"I don't know."

"But what is your gut feeling?"

"At this point I don't have a gut feeling."

This was, of course, not true, but Fors didn't want to speculate for a journalist who was sniffing around for bleak captions and big headlines.

"Thanks, Detective. We'll be seeing each other again," said Båge.

Then she went back to her car, got in, and drove off. She had just pulled out when a red Volvo eased into her parking spot. Olle Berg got out.

"So, Båge is going to do an article!"

"I don't know," said Fors.

"She's a journalist. She'll write almost anything. You know her type, right?"

"What about it?" Fors asked.

Berg had his hands in his pants pockets. He licked a small razor cut above his upper lip. "I'm going to tell you what I think," he said.

"Do that," Fors replied.

"This whole thing stinks."

"Really?"

"I ran into Nilsson and your colleague with the dog. What are you looking for anyway?"

"Hilmer Eriksson."

"I know that. I also know you've had Malmsten's boy in for questioning."

"Malmsten isn't a suspect. Nilsson picked him up because I thought he might help our search."

"That's not what I've heard."

"So what have you heard?"

"That's what I'm going to speak with your superior about." Berg leaned forward and held his face so close that Fors could feel his breath, despite the wind. "Do you know what we've just done?"

Fors shook his head and didn't back off. "Tell me."

"We've just paid an advertising agency a boatload of money to sell this town to Germany. We're launching a marketing campaign in Berlin, Munich, and Cologne. We want German tourists here. It's the last chance for this area. And now you come along."

"Yes, and now I come along," said Fors.

"Yes," Berg said. "Don't you understand what it could mean for this town if you keep digging up this neo-Nazi dirt?"

"Why would there be neo-Nazi dirt in this town?" Fors asked. His expression showed no sympathy.

"You know very well."

"All I know, Berg, is that you are interfering with my investigation in a rather serious way."

"I'm going to take this up with your superior. I know Chief Hammarlund." Berg leaned in close again. "And let me just say that if you so much as breathe a word about neo-Nazi trash to Båge or any other journalist, there will be hell to pay."

"How so?" Fors asked.

Berg didn't reply but pointed to Margit's house. "What did she say?"

"About what?"

"About her little skinhead?"

Fors didn't answer.

"Think about it," Berg said. "The wood-processing plant is going to close next year. Welux is talking about relocating. This place could be deserted in three years."

"I understand the area has problems," said Fors. "But my job is to find a missing boy."

Berg shook his head. Fors noted the dark circles under his eyes.

"Think a bit about what you could start here. What do you suppose will happen to property values if the wood factory closes and Welux relocates? It will be an economic catastrophe. Housing values will plummet. Who would want to live here? It's too far from the city to commute. We hope we can persuade Welux to stay, but tourism may be our only real option, and do you think folks will come here if our name becomes associated with the racist politics of a few bad eggs who happen to live here? Companies have to be sensitive these days. A few years ago H&M's stock tumbled when they didn't distance themselves from child-labor issues fast enough. Believe me, if we get a bad reputation, Welux won't stick around a second longer than necessary."

"I understand all that," Fors said. "But I'm searching for a missing boy. It's a different sort of problem."

Berg shook his head. "You know what I think?"

"No."

"I think it would be best if you didn't find him."

"Why wouldn't we find him?"

"I'm just saying it would be best if you didn't."

"Are you out of your mind?"

"What's done is done, right? It's not going to change a thing if you find the kid."

They were both silent for a while.

"Do you know something I should know?" asked Fors.

Berg was silent. The fight seemed to be draining out of him.

"If you know something, spit it out."

Berg took his hands out of his pockets. He kicked at the roadside gravel.

"Let's hear it," said Fors. "I know you want to protect the area's reputation, but what will happen if it gets out that a council chairman hindered the investigation of a child's disappearance—a disappearance which could very well be criminal?"

Berg kicked the gravel some more. His demeanor reminded Fors of that of the small-time hoods he sometimes questioned about shoplifting and petty theft.

"I saw some kids on the path on Saturday."

"What kids?"

"I don't know, they were quite a ways off."

"What time?"

"Around six-thirty."

"Where were you when you saw them?"

"I was wallpapering my living room."

"In your summer house?"

"Yes."

"And what did you see?"

"I heard some drunken horseplay. I went and looked out the window toward the bench. Two kids were sitting on it. A third was standing on the backrest. He was holding a can of beer."

"What did they look like?"

"Like any other kids. Dressed in black."

"Anything else?"

"My eyesight isn't what it used to be. But one of them could have been a girl."

"Why do you think that?"

"Her voice. She screamed."

"What did she scream?"

"She was just hollering. They were drinking beer."

"Are you sure about the time?"

"Pretty sure. My wife called and asked when I was going to be home for dinner. She called while I was staring at the kids. I looked at the clock. It was six-thirty."

"And then?"

"I went back to wallpapering."

"How long did you stay?"

"Until seven-thirty."

"Did you walk along the path at seven-thirty?"

"Yes."

"Where were the kids then?"

"I don't know. I didn't see a soul."

"Did you hear them while you were wallpapering?"

"I turned on the radio."

"So if there had been more yelling and noise from the path, you wouldn't have heard it?"

"No."

"Can you say anything else about the kids you saw?"

Berg seemed to give it some thought. "No."

"Thanks a lot."

Berg took a deep breath, as if he was getting his act together. "I didn't mean what I said about it being best if you didn't find the boy. You know that, right?"

"I can understand how you could feel that way," said Fors. "But what do you think happened to him?"

Berg went quiet for a time. "To be completely honest, I don't think it's good. If Hilmer was out there and those kids wanted to hurt him, he could have ended up in the river with his bike around his neck. I'm not positive, but I think the girl who was screaming out there on the bench was Anneli Tullgren and that she may have been wound up one notch too many. Nordström told me that Hilmer and Anneli had some fight at school. I'm afraid something bad has happened."

Berg muttered goodbye, then trudged back to his car and drove away. Fors stood beside his VW and looked at the flagpole. The line had stopped whipping against the pole. Not a sound could be heard from it. He thought he saw a shadow behind a curtain in Margit's house, but maybe he was imagining things. He was hungry and considered going to a pizzeria. But then he decided to see how the search at the river trail was coming along.

monday evening

nilsson's car was in the lower parking lot. Fors pulled in next to it. He got out and hustled up the path to Berg's summer house. Through the windows of a room overlooking the creek, he saw that the floor was covered with gray drop cloths. On a table standing in the middle of the room were several rolls of wallpaper, a radio, and a thermos like the kind of Alf Nordström had in his office.

Fors circled the house a few times, stopping at the side that faced the trail. The bench was quite a ways off, maybe three hundred meters. From the house it wouldn't be easy to see who might be sitting on it, especially since the view was obstructed by some birch trees.

Fors continued along the path toward the bench. After a while he saw Nilsson, walking quickly toward him.

"Found anything?" Fors asked.

"Nothing so far. The dog is a ways up. There are some large thickets. And the wind won't help the dog either."

Nilsson pointed a finger at one of his shoes and pant legs. He was wet up to the knee. "I stepped in a trench," he explained. "Chief Hammarlund is on his way from Aln. He wants to talk to you. He'll probably be here in fifteen minutes."

"And the others?"

"No one else came."

Fors told Nilsson about his conversation with Berg.

"It's starting to look bad," Nilsson said, examining his shoe.

"We need to get some divers up here," said Fors. "I'll go back and wait for Hammarlund."

"I'm going with you," said Nilsson. "I have a pair of boots in the car."

"This Tullgren family," said Fors as they headed to the parking lot, "what kind of people are they?"

"She has a convenience store. Ludvig drives a truck. He's done some time for petty stuff, been convicted a few times, for receiving stolen goods among other things. The mother makes pretty good money at the convenience store. I know for a fact that she pays tax on only every other candy sale. That store is probably a gold mine. That's what I should have, a little shop, instead of running around in the woods getting my feet wet."

In the parking lot they found the chief waiting in his dark blue Volvo sedan, which gleamed as if it had just rolled off the showroom floor. Hammarlund sat in the driver's seat with the engine running.

Nilsson headed to his car.

Without waiting for an invitation, Fors walked around the front of the chief's car and opened the passenger door. As soon as he got in, Hammarlund switched off the radio. The smell of new leather and aftershave was substantial. Hammarlund was wearing a blue sweat suit. Fors thought his wavy gray hair looked as if it had just been cut.

A racket case was lying on the backseat. At one time Hammarlund had been a Swedish doubles champion in badminton.

"How is it going, Fors?"

"You've heard."

"Tell me again."

"The boy was supposed to pick up a towel in Vallen. He took a detour to his girlfriend's house. She's the daughter of the pastor in Vreten. You might not have heard that part. Nilsson didn't know. Hilmer left the girl around six-thirty to bike to Vallen, get the towel, and return home. He was planning on watching the soccer match at seven o'clock. Everything points to him having biked along that path over there. Olle Berg, the chairman of the local council, has a vacation house a ways up the trail. He saw some kids drinking on the path on Saturday around six-thirty. Two boys and a girl. We think we know who they are. The girl and both boys go to Hilmer's high school, and the girl has a big chip on her shoulder when it comes to Hilmer. All three of them are very into the skinhead thing. They dress like storm troopers, paint swastikas, and harass immigrant kids. A month ago Hilmer got mixed up in a fight between these kids and a boy named Mahmud. Right after that incident, someone painted a swastika on Hilmer's locker. After the swastika was painted over by the school's janitor, they wrote 'traitor' on the locker. My guess is that Hilmer came biking along that path, ran into these kids, and something bad happened. I think he's lying out here somewhere. I want as many people searching as you can spare, and I want divers to look for the bike in the river."

Hammarlund drummed his fingers on the steering wheel. "It sounds thin."

"I've spoken with one of the boys, Henrik Malmsten. I played a hunch and pretended that I didn't know he'd been by the river Saturday night. At first he said that he could have been there, then he changed his story. Maybe someone else is involved."

Hammarlund ran a hand through his hair. "That's too much guessing. Do you have anything substantial?"

"No. But I can get it if you give me people."

"Where is the towel?"

"The towel?"

"Was it at Vallen?"

"I'd forgotten about it. I'll ask Nilsson."

"What's your next move?"

"Nilsson will be in charge of the work up here. There's another kid, a skinhead from the city, Marcus Lundkvist. He's probably the ringleader. I was thinking about driving down now to see him. I hope we can start diving tomorrow morning, as soon as it's light. And we need to keep beating the bushes. If what I think happened did happen, we'll find something. There are always marks or tracks. Stenberg and Johansson will pick them up."

Hammarlund seemed to mull it over for a while. "There are a lot of teenagers who run away from home. It's not even unusual for kids to commit suicide."

"Chief, this kid stopped by his girlfriend's place while on an errand for his mom. He wanted to get right back home for his favorite TV show. It's unlikely that along the way he suddenly came up with the notion of doing himself in. He ran into something or someone. He's lying out here somewhere."

Hammarlund nodded and drummed the fingers of his right hand on the steering wheel. "Be careful about what you say to the press. We don't want screaming headlines if we find out later we've been talking rubbish. Send the reporters to me."

"Fine," said Fors, getting out of the car.

When Hammarlund left, Fors found Nilsson sitting behind the wheel of his cruiser, talking on the cell phone. After a moment he snapped the phone shut and stowed it. He got out and adjusted his pants at the waist. The fierce wind tore at the birches and shrubs around them.

"Stenberg and Johansson are up by the other parking lot," said Nilsson. "They're just starting down the trail now." Fors noticed that Nilsson had changed into a pair of black boots.

"Good. Meet them at the bench and bring them up to speed. I'm going to the city to run down Marcus Lundkvist. Call me at my home number if anything comes up. I'll be back early tomorrow morning. First thing, I want to see Söderström, Johansson, Stenberg, and you at the station. I hope we'll have a diver up here by then. By the way, what happened to the towel?"

"The towel? It was hanging in the locker room at Vallen. We took it with us, and Mrs. Eriksson identified it. Didn't I mention it?"

"I don't remember. But now we know that he didn't make it to Vallen. He left Vreten at six-thirty. Then he was here about twenty minutes to seven."

Nilsson nodded.

"I'm going to the city now," Fors said.

"Drive carefully. This wind has probably knocked down some trees on the roads."

Fors didn't rush into the city. Driving gave him a chance to think about the case. And to test his hunches.

When he got to the outskirts of Aln, he ignored his hunger. He stopped at a convenience store for a bottle of mineral water, which he drank in the car.

Marcus Lundkvist's address led Fors to a group of hulking eight-story public housing buildings on a barren field. The area had not lived up to the idyllic vision of the government planners. It was a rough, squalid neighborhood. Fors had worked a similar beat near Stockholm for five years. Those years had been so bad that he had almost left the force, but then he'd decided he was too old to start a new career and got a transfer to Aln instead.

Fors found the place and a parking spot and went in. Two olive-skinned girls about ten years old with coal black hair and red skirts were sitting on the stairway in the front hallway. They stared at Fors, wide-eyed and silent. Through an apartment door he could hear what he guessed to be a Turkish pop song. Someone had pissed in the elevator, so Fors took the stairs.

Marcus Lundkvist lived on the fifth floor. Most of the doors on that floor were marked with foreign names Fors could barely pronounce, but one was unmarked. Fors knocked on this one. No one opened. He knocked again, and after a while he leaned forward to peer in through the mail slot. He didn't see anything.

A door across the hall opened behind him, and a broad-shouldered man with a large gray mustache and dark eyes looked out.

"What do you want?" the man asked.

"Police," Fors said, stroking his own minimal mustache and showing his ID.

The man in the doorway smiled. "I was also a police officer, in Tehran. Homicide. I was a captain."

Fors stepped across the hall and held out his hand. The man with the large mustache had a handshake that could have crushed walnuts. Fors took back the remainder of his fingers and pointed. "Do you know the guy who lives here?"

"I don't know him, but I know his name."

"Which is?"

"Luntkvist."

He said *t* instead of *d*.

"Ever see him around?"

"I hear him. He plays music all night. My kids can't sleep. It doesn't affect me so much, but my daughter is in the science track at school and needs her rest. I complain to the super, but it does no good." The captain from Tehran shrugged his shoulders and turned up his hands.

"When was the last time you saw him?"

"A few days ago. But I heard him playing music last night."

"Do you know if he was home on Saturday?"

"He came home after the soccer game on TV, him and several other guys. They were there for about an hour or so, then they left. They made a terrible ruckus in the hall, shouting, breaking beer bottles, and kicking at doors. Why do you Swedes make so much noise when you've been drinking?"

"We're lumberjacks from the north woods. We aren't cultured like you old Persians."

"He is bad news."

"Lundkvist?"

"Yes."

"Thanks for your help."

The police captain from Tehran shrugged his shoulders again in a resigned way and closed his door. Fors took the stairs back down. On the first floor, the two girls were still sitting on the step. One of the girls had a bag of marbles in her hand. Fors hoped they would never have to cross paths with Lundkvist and his friends. He stopped in front of the girls.

"It's late," he said. "Shouldn't you be inside?"

The girls looked at each other.

"Girls your age should be home now."

One of the girls giggled, and the other one looked dead serious. Then both of them got up, said something to each other in a language Fors couldn't identify, and scampered up the stairs.

In front of the building, Fors was met by a blast of wind. Walking to his car, he bent his head, squinted his eyes, and almost collided with Sven Humbleberg.

They stood facing each other as the wind swirled around them.

"Do you know where Marcus is?" Fors asked.

"No."

"Have you arranged to meet with him?"

"No."

"But you came to see him?"

"I was hoping he'd be home."

"He didn't respond when I knocked. Can we go to my car?"

"Yes," Humbleberg said reluctantly, and the two men walked to the VW in silence. Fors popped the locks, and they got in.

"So what are you doing here?" the detective asked once he and the principal were settled.

"I was planning on talking with Marcus."

"About what?"

Humbleberg hesitated. "I saw him on Saturday."

"Where?"

"He came to my place to borrow some tools. He'd been at Anneli's. They'd broken up."

"What time was it?"

"Just before three o'clock."

"And then where did he go?"

"He said that he was going home to fix his car. Then he was going to watch the game. I suggested that he swing by and visit his mother, but he said he didn't have time."

"And why did you come here tonight?"

"I wanted to talk to him."

"About what?"

"About Hilmer."

"Hilmer?"

"I wanted to be sure he didn't have anything to do with Hilmer's disappearance, and if he did, then I was going to ask him to go to the police."

"Would he do that if you asked him about it?"

Humbleberg paused and appeared to consider this. "I don't know. But I want to do what I can."

"What did he say about Anneli?"

"That it was over."

"Who dumped whom?"

"Marcus said that he was the one who broke it off."

"Are you sure about the time?"

"I had a meeting at three o'clock and left home ten minutes before. Marcus had just left."

"What was wrong with his car?"

"Nothing was wrong. He was thinking about installing a cutout switch so the car would be difficult to steal."

"Is he handy with tools?"

"He's not stupid. He learns what he wants to learn."

"And now you wanted to meet with him?"

"Yes."

The wind was rocking the small car.

"I called him this morning," Humbleberg said after a while. "It was the first thing I thought about when I heard that Hilmer was missing."

"What did you think?"

"That I hoped Marcus wasn't involved."

"So you thought he might have been."

"Margit would never be able to handle it if he was."

"But what made you think that Marcus might be involved?"

"Because he knows Anneli as well as Bulterman and Malmsten. But I think he went home. He seemed anxious to get to work on his car."

Both men looked straight ahead as they spoke, both had their hands in their laps. From behind them, a young man came striding by. He nearly brushed the car as he passed. The boy had close-cropped hair and was dressed in black jeans and a thin jacket.

Humbleberg opened the door and got out. "Marcus!" he called.

Marcus turned around. He had both of his hands jammed into his pockets, and his shoulders were hunched up.

"What is it?"

"Can we talk?"

"What about?"

"Come here."

Marcus took a few steps toward the car.

"Come and talk a minute," Humbleberg urged.

Marcus came a few steps closer to the car and stopped. "Who's that with you?"

Fors stepped out. "My name is Detective Fors, and I'm a police officer. I'm investigating the disappearance of Hilmer Eriksson."

"As far as I know, he's not here," said Marcus.

"But you know who he is?"

No answer.

"You know who Hilmer is?" Fors repeated.

"Are you really a cop?" Marcus asked.

"Yes."

"You guys always bother the wrong people, you know that?"

"Are you going to answer my question?"

"Are you going to answer mine?"

"Hilmer Eriksson has disappeared."

"I don't give a crap."

"Marcus," Humbleberg cautioned.

The boy turned on him. "Are you the one who brought him here?"

"Marcus . . ."

"I don't talk to pigs."

Marcus turned on his heel and stormed off.

Humbleberg and Fors watched him go.

"Can I drop you somewhere?" Fors asked.

Humbleberg pointed. "My car's over there, thanks. I'm going home."

"I'll see you," said Fors, getting back behind the wheel.

In his side-view mirror he watched Sven Humbleberg walk to his car and get in. Fors waited until he saw the red taillights of the principal's car disappear down the road. Then he got out and returned to Marcus's building.

The girls who had been sitting in the stairwell were nowhere to be seen. On his way up, Fors heard an argument through a closed door. Behind another, a child was crying. Fors stopped outside Lundkvist's apartment and caught his breath, realizing he was dizzy with hunger. He knocked on the door. After a while he thought he heard noises on the other side.

He knocked again. The door opened a crack.

When Marcus caught sight of Fors, he tried to close the door, but Fors had already wedged his foot in.

"If you'd prefer, I can come back with two uniformed colleagues," he said.

"I don't talk to pigs."

"You can decide if you want to talk with me or not. And I can decide to bring you in for questioning."

"No, you can't. I haven't done anything."

"What happened in the hallways here on Saturday?"

"What are you talking about?"

"Weren't you and some of your friends going around raising a little ruckus, threatening your neighbors' civil liberties?"

"I don't think so."

"Either you let me in or I leave. But if I leave, I'll be back with company in fifteen minutes, we'll knock the door off its hinges, and we'll haul you in for questioning. I understand you may have a few military-type items in your possession that you wouldn't want us to find."

Marcus let the door swing free and walked ahead of Fors into the apartment.

As he followed, Fors gave the place a quick once-over. In the kitchenette, on top of a gray Formica counter, sat an open pizza box. The bedroom had a mattress on the floor with a crumpled duvet, a floor lamp, and some books in a stack next to the bed.

Fors joined Marcus in the living room, where the decor did not feature any flowers or curtains. A poster on the wall showed a young man with a resolute expression. The man wore a German army helmet from the Second World War. A red horizon glowed in the background. On the facing wall hung the Nazi flag. The room was sparsely furnished with white lawn furniture, a table, and three folding chairs.

Fors went over to the window, where he had a view of his parked car. A bayonet lay on the windowsill. It was for a Mauser, a bolt-action rifle first produced in 1896. It had still been a common weapon in the Swedish army when Fors was serving.

The detective picked up the bayonet, pulled it out of the sheath, and eyed the blade. It was well oiled. "Do you carry this with you when you go out on the town?"

"I've got nothing to say to you."

"We can make this a short visit or we can turn it into a rather long-winded affair. You know that you can be evicted for what happened here on Saturday?"

"Your threats don't scare me."

"You'll have to move home to Mom again."

"Don't bring my mother into this."

"You got her involved a long time ago."

"You don't know anything about it."

"Didn't you use her keys to get into the school five years ago? You painted swastikas on the teachers' mailboxes, isn't that right?"

"You know, there's a statute of limitations on that."

"I'm not talking about the crime, I'm talking about how you got your mother involved. What did you do on Saturday?"

"None of your business."

Fors sat down on one of the chairs and crossed his legs. "Is this Margit's lawn furniture?"

Marcus didn't answer.

"It seems like you should be able to take care of yourself, but maybe you can't keep a job because you piss people off and you don't like people. So you live off Mom. And then you tell me not to drag her into this. How do you think she feels about having to support a kid like you? How long do you think she can keep it up?"

"Cut the social worker crap. Spit out what you want to say and leave."

Fors picked at a paint flake on the table with a fingernail.

"Spit it out!" Marcus warned.

"What is it that you want me to spit out?"

"You'd know better than me."

"I think you know what it's about. You know that Hilmer Eriksson has disappeared."

"I don't know the kid."

"Tell me about the graffiti on Hilmer's locker."

"I don't know what you're talking about."

"Someone's been defacing Hilmer Eriksson's locker at school. A slur and some Nazi symbols. It could have been Anneli Tullgren. I understand you two know each other."

"We broke up."

"When?"

"On Saturday."

"Did you see Anneli on Saturday?"

"That's none of your business."

"I'm asking if you saw Anneli on Saturday. Answer me or it's a free ride to the station."

Marcus glared at Fors, and Fors noted that he had blue eyes.

"What would you prefer?"

"Yes, I saw her."

"Where?"

"At her place."

"What time?"

"I don't know. Maybe around twelve."

"How long did you stay?"

"A few hours."

"Were her parents home?"

"No."

"Where did you go after you left Anneli's?"

"I went to Sven's."

"What did you do at Sven's?"

"Borrowed some tools."

"And then?"

"I drove home and messed around with the car."

"How long did you work on it?"

"Until just before six. Then my friend Rolle showed up."

"And then?"

"We went to a sports bar called the Capri to see the match."

"What time did you get to the Capri?"

"Just after six."

"How long did you stay?"

"The match started at seven. We got there around six. We didn't leave until after ten."

"Then where did you go?"

"Some of us came here."

"What did you do at the Capri?"

"We watched soccer! Are you stupid or—?"

"How many people were at the bar?"

"It was packed. We were sitting at the front, the best seats."

"So there were a lot of people who saw you at the Capri?"

Marcus glared at Fors. There was contempt in his eyes and in the curl of his lip. "The people who were there were there to see soccer. I was sitting all the way at the front and stood up every time they scored, and there were four goals. Everyone saw me."

"I'm sure they did. Why did you break up with Anneli?"

"She's in ninth grade."

"What does that have to do with it?"

"What does that have to do with it?" Marcus mimicked.

"Don't you like younger girls?"

"Get a grip."

"People like you always have a thing for younger girls. Girls who are easily impressed by beer-swilling bad boys. Anneli is perfect for you."

"You don't know anything."

"Explain it to me, then."

"No way."

Fors drummed his fingers on the table.

"Are you done now?" Marcus asked.

"Do you think I should be?"

"If you're done, you can get out of here."

"Marcus, what do you think happened to Hilmer?"

"How should I know?"

"Do you think someone hurt him?"

"I don't give a damn."

"Do you think that someone you know hurt Hilmer?"

"Get out of here!" Marcus yelled, so loudly that his face turned red.

Fors was unfazed.

"If some fifteen-year-old kids have hurt Hilmer, they'll be put in the custody of Social Services, probably for a very long time. But someone your age who's an accessory to serious assault will end up in prison."

Marcus curled his upper lip again. "You don't scare me."

"I'm not trying to scare you, I'm just telling you how things are. We'll find Hilmer soon, and if he's hurt we're going to catch the people who hurt him. Why don't you think things over? If there's something you want to tell me, you can reach me through the police switchboard. If you were involved in Hilmer's disappearance, you'll make things easier for yourself by helping the investigation. And if I were you, I'd start minding my manners around here. If you don't, you might find yourself evicted, and you wouldn't want that, would you? You have such a nice place here, a special spot to keep your very own bayonet and your motivational wall hangings."

Fors saw himself out. In front of the building he was happy to be greeted by gusts of strong wind. It felt refreshing, in spite of the clouds of dust.

When Fors got to his apartment, he went straight into the kitchen without taking off his jacket. He put a pan of water on to boil, and with a head of lettuce from the fridge and three tomatoes from a bowl on the kitchen table, he prepared a salad. After showering, he padded back to the kitchen, put spaghetti in the boiling water, and grated a large piece of Parmesan until nothing was left. Wearing the blue bathrobe that had been his last Christmas present from his ex-wife, he sat at the kitchen table and opened his mail. There were two bills and a request from the library to return an overdue book.

When the spaghetti was cooked and drained, he tossed it with butter and cheese and served himself. As he ate, he thought about Hilmer. He also thought about where his overdue library book could be. When he had finished eating, he tidied up and began searching in the living room. He found the novel under a pile of newspapers. He was standing with the book in his hand when the telephone rang. It was Nilsson.

"You're supposed to have an answering machine," Nilsson said reproachfully.

"It's broken."

"We've found him."

"Where?"

"In a compost pile behind Hagberg's, the little house with the mushrooms. You know where it is?"

"Yes."

"It was Söderström and the dog who found him, just after you left."

"Is he alive?"

"Yes, but it doesn't look good."

"What happened?"

"He's been beaten severely. He was unconscious when we found him. He's at the university hospital now."

"Make sure a photographer gets out there."

"Now?"

"Yes."

"It's late."

"Call Chief Hammarlund. Make sure Hilmer gets photographed while he's still alive. I need the pictures tomorrow. I'm going to the hospital now. We'll meet at your station at seven tomorrow morning. Before that, I want to see the place where you found him. Make sure you have enough men for arrests and three different house searches. First thing in the morning, we're bringing in Tull-gren, Malmsten, and Bulterman for questioning if they're not already at school."

Before hanging up he gave Nilsson his cell phone number. In the kitchen he opened a bottle of mineral water and drank it while looking through the window. Across the courtyard he could see a couple kissing in a bedroom. They were standing in front of their window, she in a nightgown and he in shirtsleeves. As Fors emptied the bottle, she pulled down the curtain. Fors got dressed, put his cell phone in his pocket, and went out to the car.

It took barely ten minutes for him to drive to the hospital. He hustled to intensive care, showed his ID, and spoke with the head nurse, a woman his own age, wearing green scrubs. She pointed toward a door: OPERATING ROOM B. Then she pointed to another room. "The parents are over there," she said. "The surgeons are working on the boy now."

Fors went to find the parents. There wasn't a real waiting room in the intensive care unit, so they were sitting in the nurses' lounge. On a vinyl-covered couch, the mother was leaning her head against her husband's shoulder. She cried silently, and her husband held her. He was very pale.

Fors went up to them. The woman didn't seem to see him.

"Excuse me," said Fors, who hated interrupting like this. He introduced himself to the father.

Mrs. Eriksson let out a whimper, and Fors would have had a hard time identifying it as a human sound if he hadn't known where it came from.

"He's been beaten terribly," Anders Eriksson whispered. "If it hadn't been for the shirt, I don't think I would have recognized him."

Saying this sent the tall man into a crying jag, and he buried his face in the woman's short, red hair.

"It might seem a terrible intrusion," said Fors, "but I've requested a photographer. He's coming in a while. If the doctors al-
low it, he'll take pictures of Hilmer."

Fors realized that he had been whispering.

The woman wailed.

"I understand," the man said, in a voice that was also just a whisper.

His words struck Fors. In situations like this, the detective didn't
understand anything. He couldn't comprehend how it could be
necessary to tear a boy to pieces, a boy who was interested in chess
and tried his best at soccer.

And Hilmer moved around them in the room, terrified of what he
now understood had been done to his body. He saw his mother crying and tried to comfort her. But she didn't notice him.

She didn't see him.

Around him
    the scent
    of rotting leaves.
    As if it were fall
    not May.
    Not the time of the larks
    or the swallows but the
    time of the crows.

Fors found the head nurse and gave her his cell phone number. "I
need to speak with a doctor who examined Eriksson. Could you
call me when someone's free? I'll wait outside."

"Sure," the woman in green said without looking up. She was flipping through a thick file.

Fors headed out front for some air. In the corridor leading to the unit's door, Ellen Stare and a tall older woman with long, flowing, nut brown hair were rushing in. Ellen was red eyed and pale.

"How is Hilmer?" she asked.

Fors pointed to the nurse. Then at the staff lounge. "That woman would know. Hilmer's parents are sitting in there."

As Ellen hurried toward the desk, Fors introduced himself to the woman with the long hair.

"Aina Stare," she said. "I'm Ellen's mother."

Fors nodded. "I'm in charge of the investigation, Pastor."

"Is it true that he's been beaten?"

"Yes."

"Do you know who did it?"

"No."

"How bad is it?"

"I don't know. I'm waiting to speak with one of the doctors who examined him."

Aina Stare scrutinized him. Then she quickly stretched out her hand and squeezed his arm, before going after her daughter to the staff lounge. Fors followed the long corridor toward the exit.

Outside he decided that the wind must have died down a bit. Sitting in his car, he turned on the radio and listened to music he didn't have the faintest interest in. But he didn't bother changing the station. He leaned back and closed his eyes. He had almost fallen asleep when his phone rang.

"Dr. Sjölund can meet with you now."

Fors hustled back to the large building. At the front desk in the intensive care unit, he was greeted by a man slightly younger than himself. Dr. Sjölund spoke quickly and kept his eyes focused on Fors the entire time.

"Hilmer Eriksson was suffering severe hypothermia when he was treated in the ambulance on the way here. He was hit with a blunt object. Six teeth are missing, his upper and lower lips are destroyed, the nose bone is flattened, his jaw is crushed, and the left eye is so damaged the sight is probably gone. Two ribs are broken, and one lung is punctured. We still don't know the extent of the damage to his kidneys or his spleen. He's been unconscious since he was found. He hasn't reacted to voices or other stimuli, and we don't know whether he's suffered brain damage. His condition is critical."

"I've requested a photographer. I hope it's okay with you if we take some pictures," said Fors.

Without moving his eyes, Sjölund answered. "You could put an orchestra next to Eriksson's bed and he's not going to notice it."

A pager in Sjölund's pocket started beeping. He took it out, read the display, and reached for a phone on the other side of the desk.

"Thanks," said Fors.

Sjölund nodded, and the detective left the hospital. There was nothing more he could do tonight.

When he got back home, he stripped completely, opened the bedroom window, crawled into bed, and turned out the light. He lay still and tried to think pleasant thoughts. The scent of the cherry tree in the yard drifted through the window.

Fors remembered a creek.

He had gone fly-fishing there as a kid. To get to his favorite spot, he had to leave his bike on a forest path and trudge through the woods for an hour. The creek deepened into two pools at his favorite spot, where there was always good fishing the week before midsummer. He remembered the large white flies he had used and trout that weighed a kilo.

He remembered a great spotted cuckoo and fields of cotton grass.

He remembered a pigeon hawk.

He tried to stay with the pleasant thoughts, but it was a losing battle.

tuesday morning

detective Fors reached the parking lot below Berg's summer house just before six-thirty. He parked next to the cars that were already there: Nilsson's cruiser and Söderström's, which had a caged area in back for the dog, plus one additional marked police car. A gray minibus from Forensics was also on the scene. As Fors got out of his car, Chief Hammarlund arrived in his sedan and parked next to him.

Until a year ago, Hammarlund had been a superintendent in charge of the Major Crimes Unit. Then he'd been promoted to chief of police directly under Commissioner Lönnergren, but he was still for all intents and purposes head of the MCU. He stepped out of the car sporting tasseled loafers, light-colored pants with sharp creases, a white shirt, a tie with blue and yellow stripes, and a dark blue blazer. He cast an angry look at the sky, from which a steady drizzle was falling, then opened the door of the backseat and took out a light-colored cotton overcoat. He put it on and walked up to Fors, who was dressed in the same suede jacket he had worn the day before. He had zipped it closed and turned up the collar.

"Do I need boots?" Hammarlund asked.

"Boots would be good."

Fors took note of his boss's dark blue dress socks festooned with small yellow bells.

"Do you have an extra pair?" Hammarlund asked.

"Nilsson might."

"Where is he?"

Fors dialed Nilsson on his cell phone. "Chief Hammarlund is wondering if you have an extra pair of boots."

Nilsson was slow to respond. "I have an extra pair in the car. What size is he?"

Fors turned to Hammarlund. "What size do you need?"

"Ten."

"He's a ten," said Fors.

Nilsson said he had a pair in the trunk that would do.

Fors hung up and told Hammarlund that the officer was on his way down.

The detective turned his face toward the wet, gray sky, letting a few raindrops run down his cheeks. "At least the wind's stopped blowing," he said.

They waited in the chief's car. Even today Hammarlund hadn't skimped on the aftershave.

"What's your plan?" he asked Fors.

Fors explained.

Hammarlund asked a few questions and emphasized the youth of the suspects. He was going to speak with the prosecutor.

"Who's the prosecutor?" Fors asked.

"Hallman is on Crete, Brunnberg is sick. It will probably be Bertilsson," Hammarlund replied. Then he reached into the back-seat for a grayish brown folder with elastic bands around two of the corners. He handed it to Fors. "I got this from Wickman this morning."

He peered at the clock and out the windshield as the rain increased. Nilsson materialized at the head of the path, dressed in the department's standard-issue white raincoat. From the trunk of his cruiser he got a pair of boots and brought them to the chief, who had opened the car door and already kicked off his shoes.

"I don't have any extra socks," Nilsson said when he saw the fancy pair Hammarlund was wearing. The chief took the boots and pulled them on, stuffing his pant legs in the boot tops. Fors, meanwhile, was flipping through the folder.

"Let's go," ordered Hammarlund, and all three of them headed up the path.

The bench near Berg's summer house was covered in plastic sheeting secured by blue and white crime-scene tape. Fors, Hammarlund, and Nilsson turned off toward the brown cottage with the concrete mushrooms. Fors could feel the damp seeping in through his pants at the ankles.

The whole property was cordoned off with more police tape. A uniformed female officer in a white raincoat was standing guard under a large pine tree. Nilsson pointed to the shrubbery edging the lawn at the back of the house. Behind the shrubbery was a composting enclosure. It was fenced in, with four waist-high corner stakes as thick as bedposts. The horizontal planks connecting the stakes were sagging outward from the weight of the large pile of decaying leaves and grass clippings inside the enclosure. Fors could see that the pile had recently been turned. Nilsson gave the details.

"He was lying there. Covered so that nothing could be seen. We would never have found him without the dog. I thought he was dead, but of course he wasn't. The ambulance got here right away. They had just taken someone up to Graningen, and we caught them on their way back. It took only fifteen minutes for them to get here. We covered him with every blanket and coat we could find. I went to get the parents."

Nilsson slowly shook his head. The rain on his face made it look like he was crying.

"Have you found anything else?" Hammarlund asked.

"A drag trail from the bench. It looks like that's where they knocked him down and beat him senseless. Then they probably tried to carry him, but he must have been too heavy. So they pulled him by his legs, threw him on the compost, covered him up, and went home."

Hammarlund wiped his face with a handkerchief. "Has the press been here?"

"Not yet," Nilsson replied.

"Any minute now. Send them to me when they come."

"Will do," said Nilsson.

And while they were talking, Hilmer tried crawling toward them over the wet grass, shivering from the cold. He wanted Ellen.

Where can I find Ellen? Please, take me to Ellen!

But no one heard and no one saw, because Hilmer was invisible.

Just like his hopes.

Just like his life.

The rotted leaves of autumn in his mouth.

Fors leaned over the unpainted boards around the compost pile. He pinched a brown leaf between his thumb and finger and smelled it. As the rain beat down harder, the policewoman walked up to Hammarlund; she pointed to something in the woods and pulled up the collar of her raincoat.

Fors bent forward, took a fistful of leaves out of the compost, and put them in his right pants pocket.

"Probably a moose," Hammarlund told the policewoman.

Fors circled the compost pile. "Stenberg and Johansson have gone over everything, right?" he asked Nilsson. Officers Stenberg and Johansson were the core of the city's Forensics Department. Fors had faith in Stenberg but not in Johansson.

"Of course," said Nilsson. "They even took away a piece of the bench."

"Were both of them here?"

"Both of them. They're down in the truck. Söderström and the dog are still in the woods, looking for the shoe the boy was missing when we found him."

Fors figured he had seen what he needed to. "We're going to your station."

He turned to the policewoman. Strömholm, according to her name tag. She looked fresh out of the academy.

"When the journalists show up, send them to Hammarlund. Otherwise you don't say anything. If they want to cross the tape to take pictures, threaten them with the canine unit. Is that clear?"

Strömholm nodded.

"Nilsson will send a replacement at lunch."

Strömholm nodded again. Fors saw that she was shivering.

"Then we're ready to go," he said.

Hammarlund, Nilsson, and Fors headed off toward the path. The rain increased, and when they got to their cars, heavy drops were splattering against the car tops.

Stenberg and Johansson sat wrapped in their raincoats in the Forensics Department's minibus, passing a thermos back and forth. They could barely be seen behind the streaming windshield.

Hammarlund returned the boots, and everyone drove off, with the chief in the lead. When the convoy pulled onto the main road, Fors noted a light blue car heading in the direction of the crime scene. Annika Båge, the newspaper reporter, was behind the wheel.

• • •

At the station there weren't enough chairs in the staff room for everyone. Hammarlund positioned himself against the wall while the others sat. No one took off his coat. Two more cops had arrived from the city just as the others pulled in. The driver was named Martinsson, and he was well over six feet tall. His colleague, Svan, was five foot seven. Everyone called them Big and Little.

Except for the chief, they sat in a semicircle. Big stretched out his gigantic legs and crossed them. When everyone was settled, Fors cleared his throat.

"Stenberg and Johansson will do Bulterman. Martinsson and Svan will do Malmsten. Nilsson and I will take Tullgren. All three have just turned sixteen and are still more or less kids in the eyes of the law. Remember that. We'll do house searches at the same time we pick them up. Any clothes you find, particularly pants and shoes, take with you. Make sure the kids don't see one another, much less speak to one another. If they ask questions, don't say anything except that they are being taken in for an interview regarding a disappearance. As far as we know, the kids will be released this afternoon. Any questions?"

"Where do they live?" Martinsson asked.

Nilsson gave directions with the help of a local road map.

"Let's do it," Martinsson said, and the meeting broke up.

Chief Hammarlund pulled Fors aside. "I'm going to the city now. Release them before one o'clock if you don't find anything that without a doubt connects them to the crime. Preferably earlier if you realize that it won't stick."

"It's going to stick," said Fors.

Hammarlund raised his bushy eyebrows and gave the detective a doubtful look. Then he followed the others to the parking lot. Nilsson and Fors were the only ones remaining.

"You're soaked," Nilsson said. "Want to borrow something?"

Without waiting for an answer, he went to a closet by the front door and took out a light blue wool sweater. He handed it to Fors. "You can borrow this one. It's warm. There are holes in the elbows; I've had it for ages. Socks as well?"

"Okay, thanks," Fors said, realizing how wet his feet were.

Fors took off his drenched suede jacket and pulled the sweater over his flannel shirt. Then he changed socks and put the jacket back on.

"Now you'll manage," said Nilsson. "Christ, what miserable weather for the middle of May."

"Tell me again about the Tullgren family," Fors asked.

Nilsson rubbed his chin. In his left hand he held his forage cap.

"Well, the mother, Berit, is about thirty-five. She got pregnant pretty young, and the guy legged it when Anneli was born. A few years later Berit hooked up with Ludvig. He's about ten years older than Berit, used to be a trucker. They're both big drinkers. They had their own kid a few years ago—Ulf, a nice boy. Ludvig ran a couple trotting horses for a while. He won a lot of money. Since then he's gone downhill. We've taken him in for drunk driving, and he was suspected of receiving stolen goods last year. And then there was that incident with Berit's store. He was camped out in there, waiting, and he just let loose and broke the collarbone of the uninvited guest, some dumb, desperate immigrant.

"At first, nobody around here had objections to Ludvig cooling off in jail for a few months. That's what happens when you take the law into your own hands. What made people angry was that the burglar got off with only a fine and probation. It doesn't square with people's understanding of justice. Ludvig became a local hero, and the incident whipped up anti-immigrant sentiment. Starting with the daughter. Anneli had a hard time at school when she was younger. She was overweight, got teased a lot. Then one day she just snapped. She jumped a classmate and tried to strangle her with a scarf. It was ugly. They had to administer mouth-to-mouth to save the girl. I conducted the investigation. Anneli was ten at the time. Social Services got involved, but I don't know if they did anything. The girl isn't stupid, that's for sure, but—"

Fors hung on the words. "But what?"

"I don't know, sometimes you see something in a person's eyes. You know, that look that scares you."

"And you see that in Anneli?"

"Let's just say I wouldn't let my grandkids play in the park if Anneli was there."

"She's that bad?"

"There are parents who have threatened to keep their kids out of school if something isn't done about her. She fights, hard and happily . . . I'm always getting complaints and questions." Nilsson gave a frustrated shrug. "But the ball's not in my court. I direct them to Social Services."

"All right," said Fors. "We should get going."

Each man took his own car. In a few minutes, they pulled up in front of Anneli's brick house. The house was surrounded by a sturdy wire fence with a gate that looked as if it was made out of varnished oak. The gate stood half open. Next to the door a small Swedish flag had been tacked up. It was soaked through after the long rain and hung limply.

Nilsson pressed the doorbell button, and a chime sounded inside. He pressed again. After a while the door was opened by a flabby-faced woman with light hair pulled back in a messy tangle. She wore jeans and a faded flannel shirt and held a smoldering cigarette.

"Hello, Berit," Nilsson said. "Can we come in?"

Berit cast a quick, unfriendly look at Fors.

"This is a colleague from the city," Nilsson explained with a nod in Fors's direction. "We need to speak with you."

"About what?"

"Can we come in?" Nilsson asked.

Berit Tullgren reluctantly moved to the side, and Nilsson and Fors stepped in through a cloud of smoke.

"Who is it?" a man's voice called from the rear of the house.

"Nilsson!" Berit yelled back.

"The sheriff?"

"Yes," Berit answered. "And his deputy."

Fors closed the door behind him as the man appeared in the hallway. He was wearing only a pair of red sweatpants. He was no more than five foot six but heavy and broad shouldered with a hairy chest. As he came close, Fors caught a whiff of coffee and cigarettes.

"What have we done now, Sheriff?" he said with a scornful laugh.

"Ludvig, this is Detective Harald Fors. He's from the Aln police department."

"Detective? Are you playing TV cops instead of cowboys today?" Ludvig smirked. "All right, I confess. I was the one who pissed outside the bus station last week. But I was pretty pissed myself at the time." Ludvig laughed and looked at Nilsson first, as if he was hoping for a response, then at Fors, whose expression wasn't friendly.

"Well, follow me, damn it, if you have to."

Nilsson had taken off his raincoat and laid it over his arm. "Is Anneli at home?" he asked.

Ludvig's expression darkened.

"Is she home?" Nilsson repeated.

"What did she do?"

"Anneli is suspected of being involved in a missing-persons case," said Fors. "We want to speak with her at the station. We would also like to take some of her clothes with us."

Nilsson placed his raincoat on a stool.

"Not a chance!" Ludvig roared, taking two steps in Fors's direction.

"Calm down," ordered Nilsson, and Ludvig halted. "We need to speak with the girl, and we're taking her clothes with us." As Nilsson removed a folded black plastic garbage bag from his pocket, he positioned himself between Fors and a glaring Ludvig.

"What the hell are you saying!" Ludvig yelled.

"We need to speak with the girl," said Fors. "I understand that you're her stepfather."

"Stepfather—what do you mean?"

"Ludvig, that's enough," his wife said, and laid her arm on his shoulder.

A door opened behind them, and Anneli appeared, heavy with sleep, wearing a dingy white T-shirt and a pair of light blue cotton underwear.

"What's going on out—" She stopped short and looked from Nilsson to Fors and then at Berit and Ludvig, who had both turned around.

"You're being arrested!" Ludvig said with an unkind laugh.

"Good morning, Anneli," said Fors. "As you know, we're investigating Hilmer's disappearance. We think you know more than you've told us. That's why we're taking you into the city for questioning. We would like to bring your clothes with us as well."

"Clothes?" said Anneli. "What do you mean?"

"Pants, shoes, and jacket."

Anneli couldn't hold back a little smile. "You think you're going to find some kind of evidence on my clothes?"

"They think they're on some kind of cop show," said Ludvig. "Big bad TV detectives."

"Shut up, Ludvig," Nilsson said, and took a few steps toward Anneli. He pushed past the girl and went in the room.

"What the hell, Nilsson?" Ludvig yelled. "You think you can do whatever you want because you have a uniform?"

Nilsson answered as he searched inside the room. "Anneli is suspected of being involved in a crime that led to a person's disappear-ance. If it turns out that our suspicions are wrong, we'll drive her home this afternoon."

Berit took a drag on her cigarette, which wasn't more than a fil-ter now. "So you're taking her to the city?"

"We're taking her to Aln."

"What do you mean 'involved in a crime that led to a person's disappearance'? What kind of mumbo jumbo is that?" Ludvig com-plained.

"I told you to calm down, Ludvig," Nilsson replied without even looking at him.

"I'm calling my lawyer," Ludvig vowed as he stormed toward what was apparently his and Berit's bedroom. He slammed the door behind him.

Nilsson had opened the closet door and was busy stuffing clothes in the plastic bag. In the hallway, Fors bent down and picked up a pair of black boots with dark blue laces from a mat next to the hat rack.

"Are these yours?" he asked Anneli. She didn't answer.

"They're hers," said Berit wearily.

"I suggest you get ready to go," Fors said to Anneli as he walked by her to add the boots to Nilsson's plastic sack.

There were two beds in the room, both with white comforters decorated with red hearts. In one bed a boy who looked about eight years old was lying under the covers, peeking out at the po-licemen. He rubbed his eyes and called for his mother. Berit came into the room.

"What do they want?" Ulf Tullgren asked.

"My name is Harald Fors. I'm a police officer. We're going to talk with your sister."

Anneli was in the room now, too. "You won't find anything," she badgered. "I just washed all those clothes."

"She washed them on Saturday," her mother confirmed. She rubbed out her cigarette on a saucer that was standing on the windowsill.

"No kidding," said Fors. "Do you usually do laundry on Saturdays?"

Anneli didn't answer.

Nilsson continued to put clothes in the sack. The bag was practically full.

Now Ludvig rejoined the party. "I've left a message for my lawyer," he said. "Don't think you'll get away with this."

"Get dressed now, Anneli," said Fors.

"Yes, right," Anneli yelled. "What am I supposed to wear? You idiots have all my clothes in that bag!"

"Goddamn pigs!" Ludvig growled.

"There must be something you can put on," Fors said to Anneli. "We're going now. Put something on."

"Everything is in the sack!" Anneli repeated.

"Please, you can't do this to a kid," Berit declared.

Ludvig left the room muttering.

"Get dressed now," Fors said to Anneli. "You can borrow my coat if you don't have anything else."

"Are you crazy? It's soaking wet!"

"It's better than nothing. Maybe you can borrow some jeans from your mother."

"This is crazy," Berit said. "The newspapers are going to hear about this."

"Put on a shirt and a pair of pants," Fors ordered Anneli. "We're leaving now."

From a dresser Anneli pulled out an orange hooded sweatshirt, a black skirt, and a pair of thick black tights. While she was getting dressed, Nilsson looked through her bureau and took a few more items. Fors noted the art above Ulf's bed: a poster showing the head of a helmeted SS soldier. VALKYRIE! the poster proclaimed in large block letters.

"What shoes can I use?" Anneli asked.

"Take my clogs," Berit said with a voice that almost sounded considerate.

Ludvig reappeared with a beer can in hand. He opened it and took a sip. "You should use female officers when you do something like this to a girl, you know that?" he said, and wiped his lips with the back of his hand. "I'll make sure to mention this to my lawyer, you perverts."

"Short-staffed," said Fors. "Sad but true. We don't have enough people."

"I'm ready," Nilsson said, cinching the garbage bag closed. He picked it up, squeezed past Ludvig into the hall.

"Then we're going," Fors said to Anneli. She slipped on a pair of black wooden clogs from under the hall rack.

"You're going to regret this," Ludvig muttered darkly. "Just so you know. I'm going to make sure you catch hell, both of you."

"Anneli will be back this afternoon," said Nilsson. "We'll drive her home."

"We'll be waiting," Berit spit.

"See you later, Ludvig," Nilsson said. He threw the plastic bag over his back, looking like Santa Claus with a sack full of coal for naughty children. He made his way out through the gate and placed the bag in his car trunk.

From the doorway, Fors waited for Anneli to lead the way out.

"Don't let them break you, sweetie!" Ludvig shouted, and took a drink of beer.

Anneli appeared not to hear, or maybe she didn't care. Maybe she had other things to think about.

"You're riding with me," Nilsson said when the girl reached the cars. "Do you want to sit in the front or the back?"

Anneli sat next to him in front.

"Damn Communist pig!" Ludvig shouted as Fors started his car and followed the Volvo down the street. When they passed a yellow brick house, Fors saw Hilmer's classmate Peter Gelin walking down the path toward the fence where a bike was standing.

Then they drove out onto the main road, and Fors flicked on the radio. An announcer was giving the news. Fors changed the station and found a violin sonata.

Listening to the unaccompanied player, the detective drove behind Nilsson the whole way to the city. When they got there, it had stopped raining.

tuesday midmorning

the main police station in Aln was a drab concrete box. The exterior was composed of bare walls and windows that looked like cannon holes.

Fors and Nilsson parked next to each other in the basement garage, then marched on either side of Anneli to the elevators. Nilsson struggled with the awkward plastic sack of clothes, and Fors carried the folder Hammarlund had given him.

They rode up to the fourth floor, where the Major Crimes Unit occupied small cubicles and offices along two lengthy corridors.

"Put her somewhere," said Fors. "And make sure Stenberg and Johansson get the clothes."

Anneli looked puzzled but didn't say anything.

"Let's go," Nilsson said after he set down the trash bag and put a hand on Anneli's shoulder.

Fors stopped by his office, a room he shared with Detective Carin Lindblom. The general opinion around the station was that Lindblom—a mother of three—would have become superintendent a long time ago had she been a man.

Lindblom's youngest child, Mårten, had bad allergies, and she had taken the previous day off to care for him.

"You're soaking wet" was the first thing she said when Fors came in.

"I know. Can we go up to the cafeteria?"

"Of course, but you should change first."

"I don't understand why everyone is so concerned about my wet clothes," Fors muttered.

"It's because we're looking after you, Harald. You're the only real Stockholmer we have in the unit, and if you die of pneumonia we won't have any big bad city cop to tell us how to do our jobs."

Lindblom was from a small northern town called Sorsele, and she didn't have a very high opinion of people who had grown up in cities like Stockholm. But she didn't have a very high opinion of people from the country either. She used to say that her father was the only person up there who didn't poach, make his own moonshine, and drive a snowmobile in forbidden areas. Her father had been a traffic cop until he was hit by a drunk driver trying to escape a police checkpoint. Now he was in a wheelchair and spoke with the help of a computer.

Fors got some dry things from a locker they shared. He changed.

"You don't have any socks?" he asked.

"Would a pair of tights work for you?" Lindblom replied.

Fors smiled. "How's Mårten?"

And Lindblom told him a few anecdotes from the day before.

Mårten was the result of an affair between Detective Lindblom and Chief Hammarlund. The relationship had lasted just a few months. The whole station knew that Carin Lindblom thought Hammarlund was a male chauvinist pig of astronomical proportions.

"I have to get some coffee," said Fors.

"And maybe a sandwich?" Lindblom suggested.

"Maybe even that."

The cafeteria was on the top floor of the building, and on a clear day the view went all the way to the lakes at Mon, where the escaped convicts had been caught. But not today. It was raining again. The clouds were low, and they looked as though they were lying between the trees in the parklike area in front of the police station. Fors and Lindblom sat in a far corner of the dining room. Fors had a big cup of coffee with milk and a rye roll with a sliced hard-boiled egg, anchovies, and a piece of lettuce.

And no one noticed Hilmer. He wandered the room, whimpering, frozen through. He longed for Ellen, whom he could not find.

Ellen.

Ellen.

Lindblom watched while Fors ate. "You've lost weight."

Fors perked up. "Can you tell?"

"Of course. Are you dieting?"

"Yep."

"That's great, Fors. Really great. All right, take it from the beginning but don't talk with your mouth full."

Fors chewed and swallowed. "We have the kids who did it," he said. "But we need confessions and some form of evidence."

Then he laid everything out for Lindblom. She listened and interrupted with questions every now and then.

"Your case is thin," she said when he finished.

"That's what Hammarlund said, too, but I've got a strong feeling about it. And I'm starting with Malmsten. He's going to talk."

"You know that?"

"Yep."

"Are you going to question all of them yourself?"

"If you'd been with us up there, you could have helped take Tullgren. She'll be the toughest to crack. As it is now, I'll question them myself, but I want you to sit in."

Lindblom agreed. Soon they were back down on the fourth floor, walking to a briefing room. There were a dozen chairs, a map of the region on the wall, and two memo pads on a table at the head of the room. The chairs were placed in a loose semicircle in front of the table. Fors took a seat in the chair behind the table. Svan and Martinsson were already there. Martinsson was engrossed in the sports section of the morning newspaper.

Lindblom took a seat next to Martinsson. Stenberg and Johansson came and sat down next to each other.

"Did it go well?" Fors asked.

"Could have been worse," Johansson said.

"Where's Nilsson?" Fors asked.

"On the phone," Stenberg replied.

Martinsson snorted over something in the newspaper.

"Can we get started?" Stenberg asked.

Before Fors had a chance to reply, Nilsson arrived, closing the door behind him.

"They've found the bike," he said as he took a seat.

"Where?" Fors asked.

"The diver came right after we had left. It was in the creek."

"Make sure it gets over here right away," said Fors.

"Done," Nilsson replied. "The diver is going to drop it off in the garage."

"Okay," said Fors. "Reports. Martinsson and Svan, do you want to start?"

"Sure," said Svan. "So we went to Malmsten's house. They were all up, wanted to offer some coffee, obviously nervous parents. The kid looked like he was going to start bawling, the mom was teary-eyed, too. We said that Henrik was suspected of being involved in a crime that led to a disappearance, but we didn't say who was missing. They asked if it was about Hilmer, and we told them we couldn't answer. The kid got dressed right away; we took three pairs of shoes and all the pants and jackets he had. A pair of camouflage-colored pants were hanging in the bathroom. The mother said they were Henrik's favorite pants, the only ones he wears."

Martinsson took over: "We asked if they had just been washed, and the mom said that Henrik had washed them on Saturday night and the dad said that it was the first time he had seen the kid do any laundry. Malmsten didn't say a word in the car. He looks like he's going to shit his pants any minute."

"Thanks," said Fors. "How did things go with Bulterman?"

Johansson cleared his throat. He was red-haired, freckled, skinny as a stick. He was also sexist and racist in addition to being lazy, and Lindblom liked him even less than Fors did.

"We rang the doorbell, and no one answered. We went around to the back and threw some pebbles at the window. After a while Old Man Bulterman appeared. He opened the window and hollered that he was going to call the police. We said we *were* the police and asked to come in. He closed the window and disappeared. We went back to the front door and rang the bell. He answered in just his underwear. Guys like him have no sense of decency." Johansson looked around, indignant. "There could have been a lady present!"

"It could have been me," Lindblom said. "Lord knows, I would have fainted if I'd seen a man in his underwear." Her voice was deadpan, and she kept her eyes trained on Johansson until he started to squirm. Johansson didn't understand sarcasm.

"No decency," he repeated, and moved his gaze from Lindblom to Martinsson, who had folded up his newspaper and was fanning it in front of his face.

Stenberg picked up where his partner had left off. "He asked to see our IDs again."

Johansson interrupted. "People who want to check your ID are troublemakers, it's always like that."

"Really?" Lindblom said.

"We asked to come in—" Stenberg continued.

"But first he examined our IDs like he thought they were forged. He even turned them over to check . . . to check the backs." Johansson stuttered a bit when he got worked up.

"Then he finally let us in," said Stenberg.

"Scratching his crotch the whole time," said Johansson.

"I would have liked to see that," Lindblom declared, which silenced Johansson.

"Continue," Fors said, his gaze on Stenberg in the hope that Johansson would remain quiet.

Stenberg cleared his throat. "We said that his son was suspected of being involved in a disappearance, and that we wanted to take him to the city and we would search the house. His wife was there too, glaring at us."

"She looked totally out of it," Johansson informed them.

Stenberg continued. "We asked where the boy was—"

"And the old man kept scratching his crotch," Johansson told them.

"I really would have liked to see that," Lindblom claimed again.

Both Stenberg and Johansson stared at her.

"What's your problem?" Johansson asked.

"Take a guess," Lindblom replied.

Martinsson was waving the newspaper faster.

Fors turned toward him. "Is it too hot for you in here?"

"A bit," Martinsson complained.

"Well, cut it out. You're like Marie Antoinette with the fanning."

Martinsson sighed and set down the newspaper with a sour expression.

"Continue," Fors said to Stenberg.

Stenberg cleared his throat. "We went into the boy's room. He has an air rifle hanging on the wall over his bed and a German iron cross on the bedside table, along with two knives, one of them a Hitler Jugend knife with a swastika on it and the other a bayonet. In a box under the bed we found a Meccano set, a bunch of Lego pieces, and brass knuckles. Next to the bed there was a worn copy of the Swedish army training manual.

"The boy was still asleep, even though we were pulling out drawers and shoving his clothes in sacks. The father tried to wake him, but it took a while. He didn't wake up until his dad pinched his big toe. Then he jumped like he'd been bitten."

"In underwear, too?" Lindblom asked, straight-faced.

Johansson sighed and shook his head.

Stenberg continued. "We explained the situation. He got dressed and tried to make a phone call. We nixed that and got him into the car. On the way to the city he was talkative. He wanted to know if we had taken his friends, asked the whole time if he was the only suspect. But we didn't answer."

"Is that everything?" Fors asked.

"Not really," said Stenberg. "We had to go out in the yard and get a pair of his pants off the line. They were soaked from the rain. I asked if he had been wearing the pants recently, and his mother said he wore them all the time. I asked when they'd been washed last, and she told me the boy had washed them himself on Saturday."

"Anything else?" Fors inquired.

"I think that's everything."

"He also has a rabbit," Johansson informed them. "I've never seen such a huge rabbit. It had chewed on everything; every door had teeth marks."

Johansson looked around, as if he was waiting for applause for his astute observations. Martinsson sighed deeply.

"And the forensic investigation?" said Fors.

"We removed a piece of the bench and found some stains. Could be blood. This afternoon we'll know for sure. There are also stains on the girl's laces."

"Laces?" said Fors.

"Boot laces," Johansson explained.

"We'll have the test results soon," said Stenberg.

"If it's blood, I want to know whose it is," said Fors. "Make sure you get a blood sample from Hilmer Eriksson. The bike will come in a while; I want you to look at it."

"What are we looking for?" Johansson asked.

"I don't know," said Fors. "Just take a look at it."

Martinsson fidgeted in his seat and crossed his legs. He dropped the paper and picked it up again. Then Fors told them about Tullgren's arrest. He mentioned that she, too, had washed a pair of pants on Saturday.

Johansson groaned. "I had no idea skinheads were so hygienic."

"What's the next move?" Nilsson wondered aloud.

Fors leaned back in the chair, linked his hands behind his neck, and stretched his back.

"Carin and I will question the boys first. We'll start with Malmsten, continue with Bulterman, and finish up with Tullgren. Don't forget Strömholm up at the crime scene; she needs a replacement."

Nilsson nodded.

"Stenberg and Johansson, make sure we find out about the stains on the bench and the boot laces. Check the bike. Don't forget to get a blood sample from the boy. I want everything sent to the crime lab immediately. Ask Lönnergren for help getting priority. I want answers tomorrow."

Stenberg sighed and shook his head. "They'll never do that."

"Talk to Lönnergren," said Fors. "His daughter-in-law is head of the lab."

"Really? I thought she was going to become a doctor."

"Get to work," said Fors. "Nilsson, bring Malmsten. Lindblom and I will be waiting in our office."

"Will do," Nilsson said, and got up.

"Fors, I'm telling you the lab will drag their feet," Johansson mumbled.

"Make sure they don't then," Fors said, doing a bad job of hiding his irritation.

The cops all left the room. Martinsson took his sports section with him.

the interrogations

detectives Fors and Lindblom had two windows in their cramped office. Their desks faced each other. Each had an adjustable chair and a bookshelf jammed with telephone books, police manuals, and dozens of case files in binders. They had their own telephones but shared a laptop. There was a locker in the corner in which each had a shelf for extra clothes, a few towels, and toiletries. Lindblom had placed a plant in each of the two windows. With the help of Miracle-Gro, large, green leaves obscured the view outside. There were two unpadded and uncomfortable wooden chairs for visitors in the room. One of them was placed between their desks, facing Lindblom's, and the other stood next to the locker.

At his desk Fors took a tape recorder from the drawer and checked that it was ready to go. He also retrieved his notebook from his briefcase and opened to a fresh page. When Nilsson came in with Henrik Malmsten, Fors turned the recorder on and placed it toward the front of his desk.

After guiding Malmsten into the chair sandwiched between the desks, Nilsson went out without a word and closed the door on the three of them.

For a moment, Lindblom and Fors sat back in their desk chairs and stared at the suspect. Then Fors leaned forward toward the microphone. He gave the date and time. Then he said, "This is a questioning regarding the disappearance of Hilmer Eriksson. The individual being questioned is Henrik Malmsten."

Fors paused dramatically. "Son, turn your chair toward me so you can speak into the microphone."

Malmsten did so. Fors edged the recorder closer to him.

"The interrogator is Detective Harald Fors. Detective Carin Lindblom is also present."

Fors paused for a moment and looked at a frightened Henrik Malmsten.

"Tell us your name, your address, your telephone number, and your parents' names."

Malmsten licked his upper lip and rattled off the information Fors had requested.

"You're sixteen years old, is that right?"

Malmsten nodded.

"You have to answer yes or no," said Fors.

"Yes."

"Yes what?"

"I'm sixteen years old."

"How old were you when you first met Hilmer Eriksson?"

"I was in first grade."

"Were you seven years old?"

"Yes."

"Then say so."

"I was seven years old."

"So you've known Hilmer Eriksson for nine years?"

"Yes."

"What was Hilmer like in grade school?"

"What?"

"Answer the question."

Malmsten hesitated. "I don't know what I'm supposed to say."

"Don't you know what you thought of Hilmer when you were younger?"

"I forget."

"What have you forgotten?"

"What I thought of Hilmer."

"But haven't you two always been in the same grade?"

"Yes."

"For how many years?"

"Nine."

"And you've forgotten what you thought of him?"

Malmsten stared silently at the desktop.

"Do you remember anything about Hilmer?"

No answer.

"Do you remember when you last saw him?"

No answer.

Fors stuck his right hand in his pocket, took up a handful of brown leaves from the crime scene, and let them scatter across the desk in front of Malmsten's eyes.

The boy stared at the leaves, and then his head sank down until it rested on the desktop. He started shaking, as though shivering with cold. All of the color seemed to have left his cheeks.

Fors reached for the folder he had gotten from Chief Hammarlund. He opened it and took out a large color photograph.

"This photo was taken at the university hospital this morning. Can you see who it is?"

Fors placed the photo on top of the leaves, right under Malmsten's nose.

"It's hard to make out the face, but you recognize this person anyway, don't you?"

Malmsten was shaking so much that it looked as if he might fall out of his chair.

"I need to go to the bathroom," he whispered. His voice was very weak.

Fors exchanged a glance with Lindblom. "Can you show him where it is?"

Without a word she got up and walked around to the boy's chair. "Can you walk by yourself?"

He got up, and she took him under the arm.

"Ask Nilsson to stay with him in the bathroom," Fors said as Lindblom led Malmsten through the door. Then he leaned forward toward the microphone. "Short pause for a bathroom break." After stopping the tape, he got up and walked over to the window.

The rain appeared to be easing up a bit; for a moment Fors thought he saw a spot of blue sky. With a finger, he tested the soil of the plant on the windowsill. It was damp.

Fors thought about the shocking things people did to each other. During his years on the job, he had seen bodies dragged from lakes with weights around their legs, he had encountered preschool children beaten to bits by parents who swore they loved their kids, he had sat hour after hour with criminals who had done the most unspeakable things, often to the people who were closest to them.

Don't get cynical, he would tell himself.

Don't get cynical.

And while the detective stood in front of the window, Hilmer was there, too. His presence was overwhelming. It caused Harald Fors to experience a tightness in his chest. In the bathroom with Nilsson, Henrik Malmsten felt a rush of light-headedness. Waiting for the boy in the hallway, Carin Lindblom thought about her son.

The invisible can make us dizzy, breathless; the missing can guide our thoughts.

What if it had been Mårten? wondered Lindblom. *If it had been my son, what would I have done then? Would I have killed the people who hurt my son? Would I have become someone I didn't want to be?*

Hate leads to action. Action leads to more hate.

Soon Lindblom had Malmsten seated back in front of the photograph of Hilmer. She sat down at her desk behind him; then Fors took his seat as well and slipped the photo away. Only the leaves from the compost pile remained. Fors turned the tape recorder back on.

"The interrogation resumes after the bathroom break."

He looked at Malmsten, who hung his head.

"The last question was about the photograph that I showed you just before you went to the bathroom. Did you recognize the person in the picture?"

"I don't know," Malmsten croaked.

"Are you sure?"

"Yes."

"Then I can tell you that the picture, which I'm now going to show you again, is of Hilmer Eriksson. It was taken at the university hospital a few hours ago. Can you tell me why you don't recognize Hilmer in the picture?"

The boy's lips were gray as newsprint, his eyes were bloodshot.

"I don't know," he croaked again.

"You've been in the same class as Hilmer for nine years. Shouldn't you be able to recognize him?"

"No, not now."

"Why not? Is it a bad picture? Maybe you would like to see another?" And Fors took another photograph from the folder, placing it in front of Malmsten. The boy had squeezed his eyes shut.

"Why do you have your eyes closed?"

"It's impossible to recognize him," Malmsten whispered.

"So you don't know if you recognize Hilmer even though I'm telling you it's really him?"

"It's impossible."

"What's impossible?"

"Recognizing him."

"But you've known him for nine years!"

"He . . ." And the boy's voice broke and became a sniffle.

Fors leaned across the table, his face very close to the suspect's. "Why don't you recognize Hilmer Eriksson?"

No answer.

"Why don't you recognize Hilmer Eriksson?" Fors repeated.

Now Malmsten sobbed. Fors leaned back in his chair and looked over at Lindblom.

His partner got up and made a show of offering the boy a tissue. "Here, blow your nose."

Malmsten obeyed.

"I'll repeat the question, son," said Fors. "Why don't you recognize Hilmer Eriksson in the pictures I've shown you, despite the fact that you've been in school together for nine years? Do you need to see more photographs?"

Here Fors took out yet another photo, which he placed under Malmsten's nose. The boy's tears dripped onto the picture and made it look as though Hilmer was the one crying.

"I need to go to the bathroom again!" Malmsten sobbed.

"Of course," said Fors. "But first you'll need to explain why you can't recognize Hilmer."

Now Malmsten stood up and screamed, the blood rushing back to his face, turning his cheeks ruddy. "Because he's completely destroyed!"

Malmsten swiped at his nose with the tissue.

"And who destroyed him?" Fors asked.

Malmsten was a drooling, sobbing mess.

"It wasn't supposed to happen," the boy slurred. He sat down.

Fors waited a few beats before he sprang the next question. "Who was there?"

"Anneli and Bulterman."

"Who else was there?"

Malmsten looked as if he was gathering his strength.

"Who else was there?" Fors repeated.

Malmsten gave a feverish shiver.

"I was there, too."

The sobbing was violent now.

Fors nodded toward Lindblom, who again led Malmsten out. Fors leaned forward toward the microphone. "Pause in the questioning for another bathroom break."

After turning off the tape recorder, he got up, walked back to the same window, and looked out again.

For some reason he began to think about Johansson. Why did he let Johansson under his skin? Johansson typified a "bad cop." He was lazy and lacked initiative. He was a racist, sexist pig. There wasn't a single prejudice—up to and including the one about women being bad drivers—he didn't ascribe to.

After noticing his heavy sigh, Fors shifted back to the desk, opened the top drawer, and took out a tin of mints. He put two under his tongue and stared at the pictures of the destroyed Hilmer Eriksson.

Don't get cynical.

Malmsten and his shadow were back in their places soon enough. Fors restarted the tape recorder and leaned toward the microphone. "The interrogation continues."

Fors made a point of pushing the microphone a few centimeters closer to the boy's face.

"Can you tell us what happened on Saturday?"

Malmsten looked disoriented, as if he wasn't sure how he'd ended up in this room.

"Start from the beginning," Fors said. "When did you wake up?"

"On Saturday?"

"Yes."

Malmsten thought for a moment. "Around ten, but I stayed in bed until about twelve."

"Who was home?"

"Mom and Dad."

"What did you do when you finally got up?"

"I had to get some groceries for my mom."

"Did you?"

"Yes."

"When?"

"Around one o'clock."

"Where did you go shopping?"

"At the grocery store over on Stor Street."

"Were there a lot of people at the store?"

"Yes."

"Anyone you knew?"

Malmsten thought a moment. "A couple girls from school."

"Which ones?"

"Hilda and Lina."

"What are the girls' last names?"

"Hilda Venngarn and Lina Stolk."

"Did they see you?"

"Yes."

"Did you talk to them?"

"Yes."

"What about?"

"Nothing."

"But you said that you talked to them."

"Maybe we didn't talk."

"What did you do?"

"Nothing."

"Did any of you say anything?"

"Sure."

"Who?"

"All three of us."

"But you didn't talk?"

"No."

Fors paused. "Who was the first person to say something?"

"Me."

"What did you say?"

Malmsten looked hesitant.

"What did you say?" Fors repeated.

"Whore," Malmsten whispered.

"Who did you say it to?"

"To Hilda Venngarn."

"Why?"

"Because she is."

"Is what?"

"A whore."

"Why do you think Hilda Venngarn is a whore?"

No response. Just a sigh.

"Why do you think that Hilda Venngarn is a whore?" Fors repeated.

"Because she sleeps around."

"Oh," said Fors. "And what did the girls say when you called Hilda Venngarn a whore?"

"Retard."

"And then?"

"What?"

"Was that all that was said?"

"Yes."

"So you were in the store, shopping, you met two classmates, you exchanged a few words. And then?"

"I walked home."

"You didn't ride your bike?"

"It's broken."

"Has it been broken for a long time?"

"Yes."

"How long?"

"A month. The front wheel was stolen."

"And what happened when you got home?"

"Bulterman called."

"What did he say?"

"He said that he was home alone, his mom and dad had gone to the city."

"And then?"

"So I walked over to his house."

"And then what did you do?"

"Nothing."

"Maybe you talked while you did nothing?"

"Sure."

"About what?"

"About Hilda."

"Hilda Venngarn?"

"Yes."

"What did you say about her?"

"That she runs around with darkies."

"What do you mean by darkies?"

"Scum."

"You mean kids whose parents are immigrants?"

"I mean scum," Malmsten said, his cheeks flushing.

"So you talked about Hilda Venngarn. Did you talk about anything else?"

"About the guard."

"You mean the Swedish National Guard?"

"Yes."

"What did you say about the guard?"

"That we're going to join."

"And what would you do in the National Guard?"

"Learn stuff."

"For example?"

"To shoot."

"Why do you want to learn to shoot?"

"So we can defend the country."

"Which country?"

"Sweden, of course."

"So you think that Sweden is being threatened?"

"Yes."

"By whom?"

"Freeloading immigrant scum."

Fors took out the mints, selected one, and then offered the tin to Malmsten, who helped himself.

"So you talked," said Fors, "about the guard?"

"Yes."

"And then?"

"Then Anneli called."

"Which Anneli?"

"Tullgren."

"What did she want?"

"She asked if she could come over."

"Could she?"

"Yes."

"What happened when she got there?"

"She had some beer with her."

"How much?"

"Six cans."

"So what did you do?"

"We each had a beer."

"Did you talk?"

"Yes."

"What about?"

"Marcus."

"Marcus who?"

"Marcus Lundkvist."

"What did you say?"

"Anneli told us he'd broken up with her. She was really upset. She cried."

Malmsten was now biting a nail.

"Why did she cry?"

Malmsten lost it. "I already said. Marcus dumped her!"

When he was speaking, he accidentally spit out one of the mints he had taken. It landed on the desk and disappeared among the leaves.

"So Anneli was upset. Then what did you do?"

"Bulterman's dad had some home brew. We took some and mixed it with juice."

"You drank liquor?"

Malmsten got angry again. "That's what I said!"

"You drank liquor from the Bulterman home?"

"Yes!"

"And then what happened?"

"Then we went out. The weather was pretty nice. We thought about going up to the river. Anneli had her moped. Bulterman had his bike. I rode with Anneli."

"What time was it when you left?"

"No idea. Six maybe."

"Were you drunk?"

"No."

"Where did you go?"

"Up to a bench on the river path."

"Which way on the trail did you go?"

"We went the fastest way, from the lower parking lot."

"Did you ride the whole way?"

"Anneli ran out of gas in the parking lot. She left the moped there. So Bulterman left his bike there, too. We walked up to the bench."

"Which bench?"

"The one by Berg's house."

"Did you have any alcohol with you?"

"Just one beer each."

"Were you drunk?"

"We'd only had a little. Bulterman was afraid of taking too much from his dad."

Fors penciled something in his notebook. When he had finished writing, he twirled the yellow pencil between the fingers of his right hand.

"And then?"

"We hung out at the bench. Anneli talked about Marcus the whole time. She was totally pissed off. She thought he was messing around with someone else. So of course she's going to be upset. We drank beer and threw rocks in the river. Nothing happened, except that Anneli talked about Marcus."

"Did anyone see you when you were sitting on the bench?"

"I don't think so. On the way up, we stopped at Berg's house and looked in. The old man was there doing wallpaper."

"Why did you look in Berg's house?"

"Why not?"

"Were you thinking about breaking in?"

"I don't know. We just looked around. It's not against the law."

"No, it's not. What happened then?"

"Anneli needed gas money."

"Okay."

"Then Hilmer came."

"From where?"

"From the other direction."

"How did he come?"

"On his bike. He has a new bike."

Malmsten spit out a bit of nail.

"Don't spit in here," said Fors.

"Sorry."

"What happened when Hilmer came?"

"Anneli got in his way. She stretched out her arms and screamed 'Stop!' Hilmer braked, and Bulterman grabbed the seat of his bike. 'You're not passing without paying a toll!' Anneli screamed. Bulterman said that she was right, if you had a nice bike then you could definitely afford a toll. I said that my bike was broken. 'Right,' said Bulterman. 'His bike is broken so you have to pay.' Then all of a sudden Hilmer lost his balance and fell over with the bike on top of him. He was getting up, but Anneli kicked him so he fell down again."

"Where did she kick him?"

"In the face."

"How many times?"

"Just once at first."

"What happened when Hilmer got kicked in the face?"

"Anneli screamed that he was a traitor and that he sided with immigrants and that he shouldn't give a damn about them. Then she kicked him again. Bulterman screamed that Mahmud was the one who had stolen the front wheel off my bike and why the hell was Hilmer defending the darkies. Both Anneli and Bulterman kicked him. They yelled the whole time that he was a traitor."

"Where were they kicking him?"

"In the face and the chest, all over."

"And you, what did you do?"

"I kicked him, too, but never in his face."

"How many times did you kick him?"

"Three, maybe four times."

"But not in the face?"

"No, not in the face."

"What happened when Hilmer got kicked?"

"He tried to get up a few times, but they kept kicking him down. Then Bulterman threw him down over the bike." 165

"So Hilmer was lying on top of the bike?"

"Yes."

"Was he kicked then as well?"

"Yes."

"Who was kicking?"

"Anneli and Bulterman. Mostly Anneli."

"How much was Anneli kicking?"

"Maybe twenty times."

"How many times in the face?"

"Maybe every other time."

"And Bulterman?"

"He wasn't kicking as much, just three or four times in the face."

"And you?"

"I was mostly watching."

"And then?"

"We thought he was dead and were thinking about dumping him in the river, but Anneli said it was better to bury him. She said he'd float in the river. If we buried him he'd become invisible."

"He was supposed to be invisible?"

"Yes."

"You didn't want anyone to see him?"

"No."

"So what did you do?"

"We dragged him to the little house down by Berg's and tried to get him into the basement, but it was locked. Then Anneli said that we should just dump him in the pile of leaves and cover him. The cottage was empty. It belongs to an old guy who's in some kind of home now. He used to ride around on a woman's bike, but then he got run over. I guess no one wanted to buy his house."

The boy was quiet for a while before he continued.

"We put Hilmer in the leaf pile. We covered him up so you couldn't see anything. Then we went down to the parking lot. Berg was still doing the wallpaper. We could hear music from his radio. He had a window open."

"What did you do with Hilmer's bike?"

"We rode it for a while, and then we threw it in the water."

All three were silent.

Fors took out the tin of mints, but it was empty.

"What happened to the shoe?" Detective Lindblom asked from her desk, and Malmsten spun around as if someone had pricked him in the neck with a sharp object.

"I threw it in the river."

"What kind of shoe was it?" Lindblom wondered.

"Nike," said Malmsten. "He had white Nikes."

"White Nikes," said Fors.

Then there was a knock at the door, and Stenberg opened it a crack.

"Can I speak with you a second?" he said, catching Fors's eye. After turning off the tape machine, Fors got up, went out into the corridor, and closed the door behind him.

"The boot laces," Stenberg said with a low voice. "Tullgren's laces. We've identified blood on the lace of the right shoe. There's no question about it. The shoes and the clothes are going to the lab. We've sent for a blood sample from Eriksson. They'll be able to say tomorrow if it's a match."

"Thanks," Fors said, turning his back to Stenberg and reaching for the door handle.

"Lönnergren wants to speak to you, too. I told him you were in the middle of questioning. He wants you to see him as soon as you're done."

"Thanks," Fors said again, and went back to Malmsten and Lindblom. They both watched him in silence as he sat down behind his desk and turned the tape recorder back on.

"Can I go home now?" Malmsten asked.

Fors didn't answer.

Malmsten looked to Lindblom. "I told you what happened," he implored, like a child who has eaten his vegetables and is asking for dessert.

"We don't decide when you get to go home," Lindblom answered.

Malmsten looked from one to the other with a stunned expression.

"The prosecutor will decide," Lindblom continued.

"When will he do that?" Malmsten asked, choking on the words.

"Tonight," said Fors. "You'll have to stay here with us until then."

"I have the right to go home after I've talked," Malmsten blubbered.

Fors turned off the tape recorder.

Lindblom got up and walked around the desk to the seated boy. She leaned down toward him. "You have the right not to be dragged into a cell and beaten black and blue, that's the only right you have. But I wouldn't be surprised if someone in this station forgot what you have a right to, so don't try talking to us about your rights. You should be grateful that we're good people."

She grabbed Malmsten by the hair and gave his head a hard shake.

"Calm down, Carin," Fors whispered.

"Filth!"

"Calm down," Fors repeated. "Ask someone to come and get him. I've got to go see Lönnergren."

As he paced down the hall, Fors estimated that there were twenty-five meters between his door and Lönnergren's corner office.

The commissioner was considerably older than Fors. Today he was nattily dressed in a gray suit, white shirt, and dark blue bow tie with white spots. A folded white handkerchief peeked out of his breast pocket, just so. Fors knocked on the open door and stepped in when Lönnergren looked his way.

"Close the door, please," the commissioner asked, getting up from his desk chair and pointing toward two sofas. "Shall we?"

They settled across from each other.

"I got a telephone call a while ago," said Lönnergren. "You've arrested some teenagers."

"Three."

"I understand they are suspected of assault?"

"Yes."

The commissioner fingered a crease mark on his pants before crossing his legs.

"Asp called. He found out from the father of one of the arrestees that the reason we gave for the arrest was supposed involvement in a disappearance."

"That's possible."

Lönnergren cleared his throat. "What is it that's possible?"

"That that's how we put it to the parents."

"Jesus, Harald. 'Involvement in a disappearance'? There's no such thing!"

"I know."

"Next time you arrest someone for assault you will say so, and you won't invent crimes that don't exist."

"Of course."

"You should know better."

"I didn't want to reveal what we knew."

"No, but like everyone else at this station you need to go by the book."

Fors remembered that someone else had just spoken to him about playing by the book.

"But you don't care so much about that book, do you?" Lönnergren said.

"Sometimes one slips up," Fors replied.

He remembered that it was the principal, Sven Humbleberg, who had also lectured him about rule following.

Lönnergren's face was filled with dismay. "Could you tell me what you're doing with these kids?"

As Fors mapped it out, the commissioner listened with his hands folded in his lap. His face showed no emotion. Fors guessed he would be a good poker player. But he probably played bridge, if he played cards at all.

When Fors finished, Lönnergren cleared his throat again.

"The prosecutor on this is going to be Bertilsson. As you know, he doesn't like to take children under eighteen into custody. You'll have to count on them being released, tomorrow at the latest. If you have anything that you want to play out between them, do it as soon as possible. And send the press to me. Everything gets so stirred up when the bad guys are this young."

"Hammarlund promised to take care of the press."

Lönnergren released a sour little smile, apparently meant in a friendly way. "Send them to me."

"Does it have to be Bertilsson?" Fors asked.

"I'm afraid so," said the commissioner.

District Attorney Sigfrid Bertilsson had political ambitions. His particular concern for public opinion had come to light just before Christmas the previous year. Four seventeen-year-old boys had dragged a sixteen-year-old girl into a basement storage area a few days before the holiday and raped her one after the other. Because the rapists were so young and had never been in trouble with the law, Bertilsson had seen no reason to issue arrest warrants. The next day the boys were back at school, bragging about their exploits. They caused a sensation. Already popular, they became even more so. The girl was forced to switch schools.

The D.A. defended his decision by saying that he didn't believe in stigmatizing youths in crisis, and since the investigation was over, it could hardly be hindered by the boys being set free.

By the time they came to trial, the boys had their stories straight. They all maintained that the girl had voluntarily had sex with them and that they had actually paid her for her services. The boys were slapped on the wrist and handed over to Social Services, which meant that each had a few sessions with a therapist they didn't take seriously. It was all a big laugh. Bertilsson made a lot of noise about the value of intimate working relationships between prosecutor, police, and Social Services. Soon afterward he was drafted to join an investigation put together by the minister of justice.

Fors sighed.

"Bertilsson isn't so bad," Lönnergren assured him; the commissioner knew the prosecutor from the golf club. They had the same handicap, and both of them were on the board of directors.

"Was there anything else?" Fors asked.

"Not right now, Detective. Just take it easy on the kids. We won't win any prizes by playing rough in a situation like this. Experience tells me that even rotten eggs can turn out all right in the end."

Fors nodded and made his exit.

"You can leave the door open!" Lönnergren called after him. The commissioner believed that a boss should always be accessible to his employees. That was why his door was almost always open on the rare occasion that he happened to be in his office.

Fors returned to his desk.

Lindblom was filing her nails.

"Let's get Bulterman," Fors said with a glance at the wall clock.

Lindblom put away the nail file and went out. Fors inserted a new tape in the recorder, labeled the first tape, and stowed it in the top drawer of his desk. When Lindblom returned, she had Lars-Erik Bulterman with her.

After the boy was seated, Fors ran through the introductory questions. At first, Bulterman answered readily and clearly. Then he went quiet. He didn't want to say what his parents' names were.

"What's your point, son?" Fors asked, squinting his eyes at the silent Bulterman.

No answer.

"We know who your parents are," Fors explained. "These are just formalities to get things started."

Bulterman stayed silent.

Fors leaned forward. "Do you hear what I'm saying?"

When Bulterman refused to respond, Lindblom spoke up. "He has shit in his ears. We should stick something in and poke around a bit."

"It'll be easier if you cooperate," Fors tried.

But Bulterman remained silent.

After ten minutes, Fors had had enough and moved him into one of the holding cells. Then he went and got Anneli Tullgren. He escorted her to the room and sat her down where her friend had been sitting moments before. With a new tape running, Fors went through the preliminaries. Tullgren answered all the questions promptly and clearly.

"We're investigating the disappearance of Hilmer Eriksson," continued Fors. "We have reason to believe that you're involved. We take this matter very seriously. Eriksson is in the hospital, unconscious, and according to the doctors, his condition is critical."

"Do you understand what that means?" Lindblom prodded from the chair behind her desk. "Critical condition. That means he could very well die. And if he dies, we have every reason to believe that you helped kill him."

"I kill whoever I want!" Tullgren replied.

"What?" Fors said in disbelief.

"I kill whoever I want," Tullgren repeated.

"Could you explain what you mean?" Fors asked.

"Exactly what I said."

"That you kill whoever you want?"

"Yes."

"What do you mean by that?"

Lindblom started to say something, and Fors snapped off the recorder.

"She means that she's out of her mind," his partner said.

"Hey, bitch, mind your own business," Tullgren replied, and turned her head toward Lindblom, who stood up so fast her chair fell over. With a few slashing steps she was next to the girl.

"What did you say, dear?"

"You dyke—"

She didn't get any further before she was slapped.

Lindblom bent forward and looked Tullgren in the eyes. "I didn't hear . . ."

"You dyke—"

And she got a slap on the other cheek.

"Say it again," Lindblom told her.

"You—"

Lindblom slapped her a third time.

"Now let's calm down a bit," said Fors.

"I am calm, Detective Fors," Lindblom replied. "Calm and cool."

"Why don't you sit down?"

"I'm fine."

"Go and sit down."

Lindblom returned to her desk, picked up the chair, and sat down. Fors turned the recorder back on and mentioned the time and date. He could hear Lindblom's heavy breathing.

"Let's try this again," Fors suggested. "You said that you kill anyone you want."

Tullgren nodded.

"Are there many people you would like to kill?"

Tullgren pointed at Lindblom. "She's one."

"Officer Lindblom?"

"That's right."

"Are there more?"

"Immigrants."

"All of them?"

"Yes."

"And how would that happen?"

The cheek Tullgren turned toward Fors was bright red from the slaps.

"I'm not alone."

"You mean you're not the only one who wants to murder immigrants?"

"Exactly."

"Who else wants to murder them?"

"I have friends."

"Which ones?"

"You think I'm going to squeal to a pig? You can hit me as much as you want. I'm not saying anything."

"But there are people you want to kill?"

"I just said that."

"Is Hilmer Eriksson someone you'd like to kill?"

"I'm not answering that."

"Maybe you don't know that we've found Hilmer?"

"I don't give a damn what you've found."

"We found him buried in a pile of rotting leaves."

"Do I care?"

"He's badly hurt, but in a few days he can probably tell us who kicked him so hard that he lost six teeth."

"Uh-huh."

"Were you the one who kicked Hilmer the most?"

Tullgren's head twitched. "Have the others said that?"

"What others?"

"I'm not saying anything."

"Were you the one who kicked him the most?" Fors repeated.

The girl had a sneering smile on her lips when she replied. "Why are you so interested?"

"Answer the question."

Tullgren shook her head. "You think you're good, don't you?"

"Answer the question, Anneli."

"You think you're better than everyone else because you're a big bad cop. But you're not any better than anyone else. I can prove it to you if you want."

"What are you going to prove?"

"That you aren't better than anyone else."

"I know I'm not better than anyone else," said Fors. "You're the one who thinks some people are better than others, not me."

"Bullshit," Tullgren said, and shook her head. "I could report her over there. She slapped me three times. You'd be the witness. But I bet you'd make sure she walks. That's why there are two of you. So that one of you can do whatever you want and the other can say it never happened. Right?"

"You're wrong."

Tullgren laughed loudly. "Okay, I'm going to report her. And you're going to find out that you're just as big a pig as the rest of them. But because you have shit for brains, you won't understand the consequences."

Tullgren made a gun with her fingers and shot herself in the temple.

"Shall we return to Hilmer Eriksson?" Fors suggested, ignoring the theatrics.

The girl shook her head quickly, swishing her ponytail. "No. Instead I'm going to meet with someone else so I can report her for assault."

Lindblom got up. "I'm going to go explain to Lönnergren that I lost my head," she said, and walked toward the door.

"Ask Nilsson or someone else to come in here," said Fors. "Leave the door open."

Lindblom nodded and left.

"You see," said Tullgren.

"What?" Fors asked. "What do I see?"

"Do you know why she left? Because I've beaten her."

"What do you mean?"

"She got scared. But I'm not afraid of her or of you or of all the pigs in the whole damn sty. You can't do anything to scare me. That's the difference between you and me. I'm not afraid, but you're all scared shitless, every one of you. All I need to do is open my mouth, and you crawl away with your tail between your legs. I feel only one thing for you and your damn system. Do you know what that is? Contempt."

"What did you feel toward Hilmer Eriksson on Saturday?"

"He's a loser."

"That's how you felt about Hilmer on Saturday, that he was a loser?"

"Loser!" the girl screamed. "Loser, loser, loser!"

"Why is that?"

"Because he sides with immigrants."

"What do you mean?"

"Don't be stupid."

"Explain."

"He gets involved in things that aren't his business."

"For example?"

Tullgren sighed and leaned back in her chair. "It doesn't matter."

Fors leaned forward over his desk. "Why are you like this, Anneli?"

"None of your business."

"Has nobody ever been kind to you?"

Tullgren lifted both of her hands and put them over her ears.

"Is there no one who's been kind to you, even once?"

"Stop!" the girl shouted, hands still on her ears.

She was still shouting when Nilsson came into the room. Without a word, he sat in Lindblom's chair. The girl twisted her body around. "What are you doing here, you old fart?"

She took her hands from her ears. "I want to report an assault," she continued. "The pig sitting there is a witness. I want to be interviewed."

"Assault is a terrible thing, and I'll take your report if someone has hit you," said Nilsson.

Tullgren snorted. "You're just saying that."

"No, I'm not," said Nilsson. "We can talk after you've answered Detective Fors's questions."

Tullgren stared over her shoulder at Nilsson, then she turned back toward Fors.

"Are you going to tell us what happened on Saturday?" asked Fors.

"It was a shit day."

"Why?"

"None of your business."

"Because Marcus Lundkvist broke up with you?"

She seemed stunned. "How do you know that?"

"I talked to Marcus."

"What'd he say?"

"Let's keep things in proper order: I ask the questions, you answer."

"You can take your proper order and shove it up your proper ass. What did Marcus say?"

"Answer my question, Anneli."

Tullgren shook her head, her ponytail flying.

Fors glared at her, and she glared back. "What are you staring at?"

"Where did the blood on your shoelaces come from?"

"I cut myself."

"When?"

"When I was shaving."

"When you were shaving?"

"Girls shave their legs all the time. Didn't you know that, faggot?"

"There's blood on your shoelaces. Tell us where it came from."

"If you want to know so bad, you'll have to find out some other way. Maybe it's from some damn swine I've kicked."

"Tomorrow we'll know whose blood it is. You could save us the trouble."

"Why should I? You don't believe me anyway."

"I'll believe you when you give me a logical explanation."

"I've already told you, I cut myself while I was shaving."

Fors sighed. "Are you going to tell me what happened on the river trail on Saturday?"

"No."

"Tell us so we can deal with it?"

"No."

"Was it your idea to hide Hilmer in the pile of leaves?"

"If someone said that, he's lying."

"He? Were you the only girl up there?"

"*Yes!*"

"Who were the others?"

"You think I'm telling a cop? You think so? You don't know anything, that's all I'm saying. You don't know anything. I'm not going to talk to some idiot who doesn't know anything and understands even less."

Tullgren crossed her arms over her chest, and after a while she turned her head to look at Nilsson. "I want to report a case of police brutality."

"Take her report," Fors said, putting away the tape recorder and getting up. "I'm going to the hospital."

He put on his jacket and walked out of the room. He went up to the cafeteria and had a plain omelet, some lettuce, and half a tasteless tomato. He drank a cup of coffee and watched Lönnergren sitting alone at a table reserved for the commissioner and his guests. The table was in a little area surrounded by latticework and flower boxes planted with plastic tulips. Six uniformed colleagues were sitting at another table talking about soccer. They were laughing loudly as one of them imitated a goalie missing a shot. Fors finished his coffee and headed to the elevator. When the elevator doors opened, the reporter Annika Båge was standing in front of him, waiting to get off. She was obviously going to dine with the commissioner and looked dressier than when she had last stood in front of Fors. She smiled, and he nodded at her. As she walked past, he caught the scent of her shampoo.

Down in the parking garage, he got in his car and drove to the hospital.

tuesday afternoon

t he presence of the invisible one is like a ghostly touch. We turn around: Who was that, where did he come from, where was he going?

The invisible ones stumble along next to us, legions, cohorts, armies of invisible lives. They whisper to us about their unlived lives, about hopes and longings.

And sometimes we might hear them. Then we are filled with a desire to say "Someone has lost his life, and maybe it was for my sake, so that I would be visible."

It could be me.

It could be you.

The reek of disinfectant hit Detective Fors in the face as he pushed through the revolving doors into the hospital.

In the intensive care ward, he found Pastor Aina Stare, Ellen's mother, sitting on a couch in the nurses' lounge.

"I was going to drop off a photograph," he told her after saying hello and sitting down beside her. He took the photo of Hilmer out of a brown envelope he was carrying. "Is Mrs. Eriksson in there?" He nodded toward Hilmer's room, which had cream-colored curtains pulled across the observation window.

"She's sitting with him. Ellen's there, too."

"How's he doing?"

The pastor didn't answer directly. She seemed to be lost in thought. "Henrik was one of my confirmation students."

"Malmsten?"

"Yes."

Fors was quiet. What could he say?

"I know his mother. She's a quiet woman who never says a bad word about anyone. When we started having trouble with the skin-heads and the immigrants, I tried to understand. I read a book about what a group of ordinary German soldiers did in Poland. Not SS soldiers but totally ordinary bakers, plumbers, and taxi drivers from Hamburg who were recruited into a police battalion. They were middle-aged guys, with beer bellies, and they shot Jews. The book explains the logic they used in order to shoot children, in-fants. Do you know it?"

Fors shook his head.

"First you shoot the mother. Then it becomes an act of mercy to kill the baby, because it would never survive without her . . .

"How can completely ordinary people use that kind of logic? I don't understand it. I don't understand how a boy like Henrik Malmsten could have been involved in what happened to Hilmer. Do you?"

"No," said Fors.

"But you've arrested him?"

"Malmsten and two of his friends."

"And what's going to happen to them?"

"Because of their youth, they'll probably be released tomorrow. There will be a trial in a month. If the court finds them guilty, they'll be sentenced to some form of incarceration at a juvenile detention center or probation and therapy."

"Henrik was a good boy, a kind boy, when I confirmed him."

"Yes."

"I don't understand."

"No."

"The book I read quotes another historian who said that the Nazi movement became so violent because Nazism spoke to violent people. But that doesn't explain anything. I can't say that Henrik Malmsten is a violent person. He's a child, and his mother sings in the church choir."

Fors fingered the photograph. "I promised to return this, but I don't want to disturb them. Could you take care of it?"

And he held out the photograph of Hilmer. The image of Hilmer. The way he had been. Before.

As Ellen's mother took the picture, her daughter came out of the hospital room. She threw herself down on the couch next to her mother. She laid her head in her mother's lap, and the whole of her sixteen-year-old body shook with sobs.

And then there was Hilmer.

That which wasn't Hilmer's body.

His presence in the room was so strong that it was almost suffocating.

He was there while his body lay stretched out under a sheet and a yellow cotton blanket, and painkillers and calming medicines dripped into him through a tube in the curve of his right arm.

And that which was also Hilmer was in the room, next to them. The ones sitting there were filled with Hilmer's invisibility, filled with the breadth and breaking point of his presence.

· · ·

"I'm going now," Fors said, and stood up.

Ellen's mother nodded. The sobbing girl didn't seem to notice anything.

As he passed the double doors of the boy's hospital room, Fors saw Hilmer's body, stretched out under a blanket. And he caught a glimpse of her. The mother. She was sitting next to her son and hoping against hope and praying to God, despite the fact that she wasn't a believer. *Good, kind God. Let Hilmer live.*

Her prayers would be in vain.

But even as Hilmer lay dying, she would imagine that the color had started returning to his cheeks. She would think that. She wanted to think that.

But Hilmer's body was dying. In a while someone would come and sit with her. Someone would take her hand. Someone would put an arm around her and talk to her. She would shake her head and remember that she had just seen the color return to his cheeks. And everything would be meaningless. And all that would remain of Hilmer Eriksson's mother would be a scream, which would hang around her for the rest of her life. It would fill her days and nights, her summer evenings and clear winter mornings, and she would sit one day as an old woman and remember how someone had come and sat down next to her, taken her hand and said the words that would cast her life into shadows. She would remember it so intensely because it would become a nightmare that controlled her, night after night.

And the tears.

But that would happen only later.

For now she sat and prayed to that God whom she had never believed in, and she hoped. Soon it would feel as if she didn't have anything left to hope for. But she wasn't there yet. He was alive. For a little while longer.

In the room that Detective Fors had left, Hilmer Eriksson's girlfriend was so shaken with sobs that she could barely keep her perch on the cushions of the sofa.

Hilmer's spirit was in the room, too, and he tried to comfort her.

But no one could hear his whispers anymore, since he was invisible.

"Do you want to go home, Ellen?" the pastor asked as she held her daughter's shaking body. "Do you want to go home?"

And they both got up and left the hospital. They went out to a small dark blue car with a dented right front bumper and they sat side by side and Pastor Stare drove out of the parking lot and up the road.

"I'm pregnant," Ellen announced.

They were driving behind a flatbed truck fully loaded with pine timber. The sharp smell of resin came in through the open window on Ellen's side of the car.

"Hilmer?" her mother whispered.

Ellen bent her head, and they were quiet together, sharing a kind of communion.

Ellen finally spoke. "That's what I told him when I asked him to come by on Saturday . . . If I hadn't asked him to come, this wouldn't have happened."

She wept. Her mother said, "It's not your fault, Ellen."

"But if I hadn't asked him to come, then he wouldn't have run into them."

"That's not the way it works," her mother said.

"I should have waited to tell him."

"It's not your fault, Ellen."

And they both were quiet again. While they sat next to each

other in the car with the dented bumper, Detective Harald Fors returned to the police station.

Lindblom met him in the hallway. "They just called from the hospital. Hilmer Eriksson is dead. He died a little while ago."

Fors shook his head. "But I was just there."

"In any case, he's dead now," said Lindblom.

"Get Tullgren," Fors snapped.

Then he went into the office, took off his suede jacket, and stood waiting by the window. *It looks like the weather is improving,* he thought.

At the rectory in Vreten, Ellen and her mother came in through the kitchen door just as the phone rang. The news brought both mother and daughter to tears again. Ellen collapsed on the living room couch. After a while she didn't have the strength to cry anymore.

Then Hilmer found her, with what was left of his strength. The very last of it. He lay down beside her. He was there with her, and in her womb.

And Ellen said: "Now that he's dead, I can't get rid of it. I can't take away the only thing that's left of him."

Outside the rectory window, it got a little brighter as the May sun pushed through the clouds.

A while later, Ellen walked out into the garden wrapped in her mother's winter coat. She walked to the edge of the woods behind their home, and she remained standing there, too tired to cry. At her feet there were some spring leaves sprouting around a cowslip blossom. She bent down and picked a leaf and put it inside her shirt, and she felt the damp from the leaf against her skin.